SECRETS OF THE PAST

SECRETS OF MUSTANG ISLAND
BOOK THREE

SYLVIA MCDANIEL

Families tore them apart. Fate just brought them back together.

Twenty years ago, Nicole Laurent's world shattered with a single email. Her marriage to Tripp Masterson ended in heartbreak, leaving her with nothing but unanswered questions.

Now she's a fierce prosecutor, facing the only man she ever loved across the courtroom. But as the trial unfolds, buried secrets rise to the surface—secrets that prove their breakup may not have been their choice at all.

Families lied. Loyalties twisted. And the betrayal that tore them apart runs deeper than either imagined.

With passion still burning and enemies close at hand, Nicole and Tripp must decide—can love survive the truth, or will the secrets of the past destroy them all over again?

Your next binge-worthy romance is free—just sign up and start reading.
https://sylviamcdanielauthor.substack.com/

Secrets of Mustang Island
Secrets of a Summer Place
Secrets of a Runaway Bride
Secrets From the Past
Secrets of a Reckless Life
Secrets of a Hidden Life
Secrets of a Midnight Letter

Secrets of Mustang Island Novellas
The Summer I Loved You
When We Meet Again
Christmas at Mustang Island

Love books? Love deals? Love a little mischief? Sign up for
my Substack—it's free!
Click Here to join

ustang Island, Texas – June 1999

Nicole Reyes had never worn a pair of high heels in her life until tonight. Her toes were pinched, her feet ached, and her dress clung too tightly around her ribs. But none of that mattered. Not really.

Because tonight, she was going to marry Dustin "Tripp" Masterson.

She glanced sideways at him, the boy she'd loved since she was sixteen. He was tall with dark hair and big brown eyes that glittered when he gazed at her. He looked too perfect in his navy blazer and khakis, like he belonged in a Ralph Lauren ad instead of this over-decorated country club on the edge of Mustang Island.

He turned toward her with a warm smile, the kind that always made her heart stumble.

"You okay?" he whispered.

"Yeah," she breathed, even though she wasn't. Not entirely.

Yesterday, they'd walked across their high school graduation stage. Everyone had cheered. Her mother had cried. His mother hadn't even clapped.

Now here they were, two kids standing in the middle of a crowd full of expectations and champagne flutes, pretending to belong, when they both knew they didn't.

Their time together was running out, and Tripp's mother couldn't be happier.

Tripp's parents had made it crystal clear: end things with the poor girl from the wrong side of town, or lose your college money.

And even her parents, who had once smiled warmly when he visited their tiny home, had started pushing her toward the future. College. Independence. Forgetting Tripp.

But she couldn't forget him. She didn't want to.

She looked up into his golden brown eyes, fear bubbling up inside her. "Are you sure?"

He didn't hesitate. "Yeah. Are you?"

She swallowed hard, her heart pounding. She loved him like she loved the air in her lungs. Like she loved the ocean. Like she loved the sunrise on Mustang Island when everything was quiet and full of promise.

"Yes," she whispered. "But your parents…"

"They'll be furious," he admitted, his voice steady. "But what can they do?"

She blinked at him. "Disown you?"

"They've already threatened to."

"They threatened to cut off your tuition if you didn't go to Baylor."

"I know."

Nicole winced. "You told them you wanted to go to UT with me. That we were going to law school together. That we had plans—"

"They didn't care. What is more important? Money or being with you? I think you're the most important person in my life, and hopefully they'll come around."

But what if they didn't? Nicole couldn't imagine not speaking to her family again. Even for Tripp, she'd have a hard time letting them go.

"Tripp..." Her voice broke slightly. This was such a drastic step, and yet, the thought of living without him was terrifying.

He reached for her hand and gave it a firm squeeze. "My mom wants to control everything. My dad... sometimes I think he lets her because it's easier. But this is our life, Nic. Not theirs. We said we'd be together. We made a promise to one another."

They had. A thousand promises whispered under moonlight and kissed into skin. They'd talked about opening their own firm one day. *Masterson & Reyes*, or *Reyes & Reyes*, depending on who passed the bar first.

But those dreams felt fragile now, like paper boats in a storm. Beautiful, hopeful, and easily torn apart. She was used to being poor, but Tripp had grown up in luxury. If he were disinherited, could he take the pain of living without money?

"Just to be clear," she said, lifting her chin, "you're transferring to Austin in December?"

Before she took this very important step with Tripp, she wanted to make certain that they agreed on everything.

"Yes. I'll finish the fall semester at Baylor and switch. We'll only be apart for a few months. I'll come see you every weekend."

"And we'll get an apartment together."

"I've already looked online. There are student places near campus."

Her heart bloomed with warmth. She was scared, but not of him. Never of him. She was more afraid of losing him.

"You know everyone's going to assume we're pregnant."

It was true, and yet, part of her didn't care. They would know the truth. They had married because she couldn't live without him.

Tripp grinned. "Well, we're not. No babies until after law school."

"Agreed," she laughed. "But... I did buy a nightgown for tonight."

He groaned dramatically and pulled her closer. "Let's leave now before I die from anticipation."

Nicole let out a breath of relief filled with a small bit of terror. They had yet to consummate their relationship and were waiting until tonight, when they were man and wife.

"Thank God. I keep expecting your mom to burst in here and drag me out by the hair."

His mother hated her and had let her know her feelings months ago. Suzanne Masterson didn't think she was good enough for her son.

He kissed the side of her head. "We've made our appearance. That's enough."

"You're certain? It's your party," she said.

"I didn't want this party. My mother did," he said as he took her hand and pulled her toward the door.

They began weaving toward the exit, trying to avoid any parental radar, when a familiar figure stepped into their path.

"Where are you two sneaking off to?" Paige asked, arms crossed and one perfectly sculpted eyebrow arched. Her silver heels gleamed under the chandelier light.

Nicole smiled. "It's a secret."

Her best friend knew of their planned elopement. She had tried to talk her out of doing this, but Nicole loved Tripp, and they wanted to stay together. Yes, it would be hard, but love would keep them together.

"Oh no," Paige whispered, her voice catching. "You're doing it. You're actually doing it."

Nicole nodded, and Tripp wrapped an arm around her waist.

"We have to go. The chapel closes at ten."

Paige looked between them and sighed. "Do you need a witness?"

Tripp shook his head. "No. You need to stay. If you disappear, my mom will know something's up."

Paige's mother and Tripp's mother were best friends. If they began to suspect anything, they would drag Paige into it and probably even torture her until they learned the truth.

"Where are you staying tonight?"

"That's top secret," Tripp said.

Paige rolled her eyes. "Fine. But use protection. Please. You two are way too young to be raising a baby."

Nicole laughed nervously. "No worries there. Just love and college for now."

Paige hugged her tightly. "You're crazy. But maybe crazy in love."

Yes, she knew she was taking a huge risk with Tripp, but she loved him.

Paige turned to Tripp and jabbed a finger into his chest. "Don't screw this up."

"I won't," he said quietly.

They slipped out the side door, away from the string lights and laughter and into the warm coastal night.

Tripp's Mustang purred to life, and they drove in silence for a few minutes, the weight of what they were about to do pressing in from all sides.

Nicole stared out at the dark sea beside the road. "Do you think we'll make it?"

He took her hand. "I don't think. I know. We love each other. We're going to be happy. I guarantee it."

When they arrived at the small chapel, the inside

smelled like lavender and old wood. Candles burned softly on the altar.

They stood at the altar, hands entwined, hearts pounding, gazing at each other.

"How old are you?" the pastor asked Nicole.

They had come this far; she had to convince him.

"I'm eighteen. I just graduated from high school."

The man frowned. "You're awfully young."

They gazed at one another.

"I'm pregnant," she said. "We want to keep our child, and our families will make us get an abortion."

The man shook his head. "All right."

She wore her sundress and the white veil she'd hidden under her bed for two months. Tripp looked at her like she was the only thing that existed in the universe.

When they spoke their vows, her voice trembled. His didn't.

"I promise," he whispered, "that nothing and no one will ever come between us. Until death do us part."

Nicole's eyes filled with tears. "Together, we are invincible."

They kissed, and the world shifted. They were husband and wife, until death did they part.

After they signed the marriage license, they ran out of the chapel, laughing.

It was done. Not the wedding she'd dreamed of, but that didn't matter. They were together, and soon, they would be attending college.

"I love you," Tripp said.

Nicole sighed and kissed him. "I love you. Let's go celebrate our wedding night."

Tripp grinned at her and started up the Mustang. "I can't wait a moment longer."

THE BANGING on the door rattled the tiny house. Maria Reyes sat bolt upright in bed, her heart clenching, sending up a prayer that all her children were safe and sound in their beds.

"Dios mío," she whispered. "Who's knocking like that at this hour?"

Francisco swung his legs over the bed and reached for the nearest shirt and pants. By the time he opened the door, Suzanne and George Masterson were already halfway inside.

"What the hell?" he muttered.

"We need to talk," George said, brushing past him, beginning to pace the floor of their small home.

"What's going on?" Maria asked, stepping into the living room. Instantly afraid that something bad had happened to her daughter and that boy she thought she couldn't live without.

Suzanne's voice was ice. "Your daughter has trapped our son."

Maria blinked. "Excuse me?"

Nicole would never trap a boy. The woman was high-society loco.

"They eloped," George said. "They're probably married by now."

"No." Maria's knees went weak. "Nicole would've told us. She's leaving for school in a month. How do you know they eloped?"

Oh God, she hoped and prayed they had not gotten married. She hoped and prayed that she was not pregnant.

The woman wore evening clothes and looked completely out of place in their modest home.

"Because I questioned Paige and she finally told me the truth," his mother said. "She said they were eloping because we've been trying to get Dustin to end his relationship with your daughter."

Oh, Maria had known his mother was a snotty bitch the moment she'd met her. The woman gazed down her long, perfectly shaped nose at Maria, and she had to resist the urge to keep from breaking it.

"And we've been trying to make our daughter see that your family is not a good fit for her," Francisco said.

The woman rolled her eyes at him.

"She's pregnant, obviously," Suzanne said with such utter disgust that it was all Maria could do not to slap the woman. "Why else rush into marriage at their age?"

"She's not," Maria said automatically, but the words felt thin. What if she were?

Maria watched George Masterson frown at his wife, as if signaling her to shut up, but the woman had a sharp tongue, and she wouldn't be quiet.

"Why else rush into this? Unless she's trapping him for our money?"

Good grief. Was everything about money with this crazy woman? Maybe she needed to lose some of her precious cash.

George ran a hand through his hair. "Look. We all can agree that this marriage can't happen. Our kids are making a mistake."

Francisco crossed his arms. "Yes, we agree. He's not good enough for her."

Oh, how Maria loved this man.

Suzanne sputtered.

"Our daughter is brilliant," Maria said. "She has a full scholarship. She's going to be a lawyer. She doesn't need a husband."

Especially, that boy. He was nothing but trouble.

"Then she doesn't need to ruin her life chasing my son," Suzanne snapped.

"Your son is the one chasing her," Maria said. "I've seen the way he looks at her."

"We're not here to argue," George said, exasperated. "We're here to fix the problem – our kids getting married."

Spoken like a true lawyer.

They all stood in tense silence. Maria was not going to offer them a chance to sit down. She'd seen the way Suzanne had gazed at their furniture. She could stand all night in her spiky heels for all she cared.

"She's seventeen," George said. "The marriage isn't valid without parental consent."

"We didn't sign anything," Francisco said. "I would've said no."

Absolutely, they would have told Nicole no and probably locked her in her room.

"Then we file for an annulment."

"And keep them apart," Suzanne added.

Deep in her heart, Maria knew that would not be enough to keep these two kids separated. "Not enough. Once they leave for college, they'll get in touch with one another."

It was true, she knew her daughter, and the girl kept saying she was going to be a lawyer, and Maria could see that stubborn determination in her child. And these two would find a way to be together.

"Not if we're smart," George said. "We're taking Tripp to Europe in the morning. No contact. No phones. It will look like he abandoned her."

These two must never have experienced true love.

"She'll still wait for him," Maria said softly. "She loves him."

Maria knew that look in her daughter's eyes. It was the same way she'd felt about Francisco all those years ago. It was young love, and it was dangerous.

"Love. Those kids don't know the meaning," Suzanne said.

Maria glanced at Suzanne and glared at her. Nicole was her pride and joy, and she didn't deserve the hatred radiating from this woman.

"We have to end this permanently," Suzanne said.

"Another woman," George said.

"Another man," Francisco said.

"A realization that he doesn't love her," Suzanne replied.

"The realization that he's not good enough for her," Maria said.

There was a moment of silence as they all stood there thinking about how to put their plan into action.

"What if Tripp were to send her an email saying that he realizes they've made a mistake. That he wants to spend his college years chasing other women," George said.

"Why does it have to be Tripp's fault? Why can't Nicole do the breaking up?" Suzanne said. "Our son has put up with so much."

Her son had put up with what? He'd married her daughter, taken her virginity, and now he was going to break her heart. Thank goodness, the parents were ending this marriage, because her daughter deserved a much better family. One that would see her brilliance and appreciate her.

"What if we do an email from each one. You send one from Nicole to Tripp, and we'll send one from Tripp to Nicole," George, the practical one, said. "Can you get into your daughter's email?"

That was one thing that Maria had insisted on with all her children. Occasionally, she glanced at their emails and texts to ensure they were safe.

"Yes, I can get into Nicole's email," she said. "What about you? Can you get into your son's?"

"Yes," George said. "He doesn't know it, but I can. So here's the plan. We'll each send an email from the other one saying that they've had second thoughts. Then we're going to whisk our son off to Europe until he goes to college. By then, your daughter will be in school."

Shaking her head, Maria knew they were missing out on the opportunity to help Nicole. "No. I'm not going to do this. We'll just let the kids work things out between themselves."

Francisco glanced at her like she was crazy.

George sighed and shook his head. "I'll give you fifty thousand dollars to help with your daughter's education and to keep her away from my son."

They were desperate. And that's what Maria wanted to hear. "Make it seventy-five and you have a deal."

Suzanne gasped. "Trash. You're nothing but trash."

It was all Maria could do to keep from yanking the woman's hair out, but instead she smiled at her. The woman was going to lose some of her precious gold and Maria would use it to help her daughter get through school.

"And you're going to be so lucky that our trashy daughter is not going to be in your family."

Nicole had received a full scholarship, but this would cover everything and then some.

"We'll send messages, one from each family. Make them both believe the other had second thoughts."

Maria stared at the floor. "And they'll never know?"

"No," Suzanne said. "It'll be like it never happened."

Maria closed her eyes.

"I want the money agreed to in writing. A contract."

"You'll have it by the morning."

Was she being mean? Yes, but in the long run, it would help Nicole. She was doing this for her daughter. Now her education would be paid for. And she had saved her from this horrible family.

"I'll get the contract drawn up and the annulment started," George said. "We'll be leaving for Europe tomorrow. By the time we get back, the kids will be in separate schools and have new friends."

With a sigh, Tripp's parents walked to the door.

Thank goodness, they were leaving, never to darken their door again.

"Let's hope this is the last time we have to meet over our children," Suzanne said.

"Don't ever come back here," Maria said. "We don't want your family here."

Tripp's parents walked out. Maria closed the door.

Francisco sighed. "What have we done?"

"Saved our daughter from that family," Maria said.

She stood in the room long after they'd gone, staring out into the moonlight, clutching her robe, wondering where her daughter was. She thought about her husband Francisco. Their own start had been rocky and yet, she loved him with her heart and soul. Had she just robbed her daughter of that kind of love?

"We just sold our daughter's heart," she whispered, guilt ripping through her.

What if her own parents had done this to her and Francisco? How would she have felt?

CHAPTER 2

Twenty Years Later

Nicole Reyes was going to bury this bastard. Derrick Reddick.

The man accused of gunning down his pregnant girlfriend, Bianca Laurent, in cold blood. A girl with whom Nicole resonated, as the young woman had just received her admittance letter to law school. The young woman who loved a man from a very wealthy family – a family who wanted him to marry someone with a pedigree like his. Not a young woman whose family was middle-class.

There was so much about this case that left her cringing inside with the realization this could have been her. Only Tripp wasn't a murderer.

Nicole had built her entire case piece by piece, with meticulous precision. She had the motive. She had the means. And she had enough circumstantial and forensic evidence to put Derrick behind bars for the rest of his miserable life.

Today was only the pre-trial, but the weight of the case already hung in the air like a summer storm. The media would be watching. The town hanging on every word as a very prominent family and a middle-class Catholic family with strong ties in the community awaited justice. One had lost a loved one, and the other would soon lose their son, if she had anything to do with it.

She didn't care.

Let them watch her win.

Nicole's heels clicked sharply against the marble floor of the courthouse hallway as she strode toward Courtroom 2B, briefcase under her arm, coffee in hand, jaw set with determination. Her dark green blouse was tucked into high-waisted slacks, her blazer tailored to perfection, her dark hair swept into a smooth, professional chignon.

The fisherman's daughter had come home with a law pedigree. No longer was she the girl from the poor side of town. Her life now pulsed with purpose, supported by a salary that allowed her to savor the comforts she once only dreamed of.

She had returned to Mustang Island to care for her aging parents. What she hadn't expected was to step right into a trial this high-profile, or one this personal. But this trial gave her something she hadn't felt in years, a purpose, a reason to face the town that had once shattered her heart.

When she entered the courtroom, Craig Allen, her second chair and longtime mentor, was already seated at the prosecution's table, scanning his notes. He glanced up as she approached.

"Morning, Reyes."

She slid into the first chair beside him. "Morning, Allen."

"Ready to wreck this guy's life?"

"Absolutely." She peeled the cap off her coffee and took a steadying sip. "Let's nail him to the damn wall."

A shuffle of movement across the aisle made her glance toward the defense table.

And just like that, the breath caught in her lungs.

No.

No. No. No.

Sitting at the defense table, looking infuriatingly sharp in a navy suit, his tie slightly loose like he never really needed to try, was Dustin "Tripp" Masterson.

Her ex-husband.

Her high school sweetheart.

The boy who'd vowed to love her forever, and shattered her heart less than forty-eight hours after they'd said "I do."

Her stomach dropped. Her pulse roared in her ears.

"What the hell?" she whispered. "He's not Victor Lawson."

Allen leaned in. "Something wrong?"

She forced a smile, her jaw clenching. "I know the defense counsel. And he's not Victor Lawson."

"Victor had a heart attack. I guess this is the new guy. Is there a problem?"

Now she understood why he was here. His name had not been on any of the pretrial motions.

"We were... close. A long time ago."

"Need to recuse yourself?"

"Not a chance!"

This was her case. Her courtroom. Her win.

She wasn't about to let Tripp Masterson walk in here and take that from her.

Not again. Her freshman year wasn't defined by textbooks or exams, but by the ache of losing the boy who vowed to love her forever... and left her within a single day.

Craig smirked. "Everyone knows the Masterson family around here."

Oh yes, she knew the Masterson family very well. A father ruled by a wife who could make the Wicked Witch look like a saint, a woman steeped in venom, with more vile than anyone she'd ever known, and one she prayed would stay gone from her life forever.

She had heard that Tripp's father had passed away recently, and her first thought had been, did his wife kill him? Too bad his witch of a mother was still alive.

"And not in a good way," Nicole muttered. "Talk about a family full of drama-filled divas."

He chuckled, flipping through his file.

"Bad blood?"

"You could say that," she said.

Their past was steeped in more bad blood than she

cared to confess, betrayal, lies, and a runaway groom. She told herself he must have gotten cold feet. And still, she couldn't forget their wedding night, so sweet, so unrepeatable, that no one else had ever come close.

Across the aisle, Tripp finally looked up. Their eyes locked.

And just for a moment, the world narrowed to the space between them.

All the memories of them as kids surged through her, only to end with that final morning after their wedding, the morning he never came back. She'd waited for hours, dread coiling tighter with every minute. And when the truth finally came, it wasn't with words spoken face-to-face, but with an email, cold, distant, final.

His lips parted slightly. Recognition hit him like a slap.

Then disbelief.

Then something else, something she didn't want to name.

Nicole turned away, stone-faced.

She didn't have time for this. Not here. Not now.

The door at the front of the courtroom opened.

"All rise," the bailiff called. "The Honorable Judge Carlton Price presiding."

Everyone stood as Judge Price, a tall, silver-haired man with kind eyes and a reputation for fairness, took the bench.

Nicole straightened her spine.

This wasn't about Tripp. This was about justice.

This was about Bianca Laurent.

About the life Derrick Reddick had snuffed out without remorse. A man who had killed his own child, along with its mother.

And she wasn't about to let him get away with it. Any more than she'd let Tripp off the hook for abandoning her, leaving her to break the news of their marriage to her parents alone. He'd promised he'd be back. He never was. And when she showed up at his house, he was gone.

As in forever gone.

The pre-trial began.

"Nicole Reyes, for the prosecution," she said, standing and facing the judge.

Tripp stood, his voice cool and confident as he faced the judge. "Your Honor, I'm replacing attorney Victor Lawson, who is in the hospital. The defense moves to suppress the prosecution's claim that this was a premeditated act."

Nicole stood just as smoothly. "Your Honor, the prosecution intends to prove that Derrick Reddick planned the execution-style murder of Bianca Laurent from the moment he learned she was pregnant."

"Objection," Tripp said quickly. "Prejudicial speculation."

Judge Price looked from one to the other. "Overruled. Proceed, Ms. Reyes."

Nicole gave a slight nod. Score one.

Her partner, Craig, stood next. "Your Honor, we

request to include the defendant's prior assault charges involving Miss Laurent. They're directly relevant."

Tripp's voice sharpened. "Objection. Prior offenses are not part of this trial."

"Including an arrest for beating the victim just three months prior?" Craig challenged.

The judge held up a hand. "Sustained. The court will not consider prior offenses unless directly linked by evidence. Move on."

Tripp exhaled slowly, giving Nicole a sidelong glance. She ignored him.

"You all right?" Craig murmured as he sat back down.

"I'm fine," Nicole said through clenched teeth. "Don't worry about me. I've been prepping for this case since I returned to the island. I just didn't prep for... him."

Across the room, Tripp rose again. "Your Honor, the defense demands that the prosecution hand over all remaining forensic reports."

Nicole stood again. "Already done, Your Honor."

"I haven't received the autopsy report," Tripp said, eyebrows raised.

Bullshit. If she wouldn't land herself in contempt, she'd say it straight to the judge's face. But for now, some truths had to stay unsaid.

Her office had sent the report the moment it was finalized. He was either stalling or trying to bait her. Either way, she wasn't biting.

"A *second* copy will be delivered this afternoon, via

courier. We will expect a signed signature," she replied curtly.

The next thirty minutes blurred into legal ping-pong, motions, objections, and clarifications. Once or twice, the heat between Nicole and Tripp threatened to override the legal decorum of the room.

They were volleying like it was Wimbledon, each trying to trip the other up, to make them stumble, to get even for the hurt left behind twenty years ago. It was less a trial and more a game: push every button, hit every nerve, and see who cracked first.

And it damn sure wouldn't be her.

Judge Price finally raised a hand.

"Counselors," he said dryly, "this isn't a tennis match. Let's keep it civil. Trial date is set for one week from today."

Craig snorted quietly. Nicole didn't smile.

Because this wasn't civil.

This was personal.

And she was still burning. Still waiting to get even.

When the session finally adjourned, Nicole packed her briefcase with swift, practiced movements.

She leaned toward Craig. "I've got to go."

"Want me to run interference?"

She shook her head. "Just get me five seconds of a head start."

As soon as Judge Price stepped off the bench and into his chambers, she made for the exit, heels clacking a steady beat against the floor.

Behind her, she heard her name.

"Nicole, wait."

Her blood went cold.

She didn't stop.

Didn't turn around.

Didn't let him see her face.

There would be no reunion, no swapping stories about wives, children, or the missing twenty years that had stretched between them. She hit the hallway, shoved through the doors, and made a beeline for the women's restroom.

Only once she was inside, alone in the stall, did she let herself breathe.

He was here.

Tripp.

After all these years.

The man who'd married her in a moonlit chapel when they were just teenagers. The man who'd promised her forever... and then walked away like it had never meant anything.

She still remembered the email.

Cold. Distant.

"I don't think we should talk anymore. I need to focus on school and move on. I want to chase women in college and not be tied down. Please don't call me."

She hadn't.

Years had passed before the hurt dulled, before she could breathe without feeling the sting. But when it came to men, trust remained beyond her reach. The day the truth hit, she shredded her wedding dress and buried the tatters, determined to bury the memory with it.

Until now.

By the time she left the courthouse and reached the sidewalk outside her office, the heat of the afternoon sun had already made her blouse cling to her back.

She was ten steps from the door when she heard his voice behind her.

"Forever looks really good on you."

Nicole froze.

The words hit like a fist to the spine. The son of a bitch.

Slowly, she turned.

There he stood. Taller. Older. Still beautiful, damn him. But something in his face had changed; there was a weight there now. A shadow in his eyes.

"Partying at college didn't seem to hurt you," she replied, her voice tight.

A flicker of confusion crossed his face. "College was twenty years ago."

"And forever was twenty," she said coldly. "But for you, it barely lasted twenty-four hours."

He took a step forward. "You never returned my calls."

"You never called."

"I left you twenty messages at least."

Nicole blinked. "I never got any."

His eyes narrowed. "And what about the email you sent me?"

She stiffened. "What email?"

"The one that said you didn't want to hear from me again. That you'd made a mistake."

Her throat closed. What had happened?

"I never sent any emails to you after you dumped me. I received one from you, saying you wanted to chase women and party."

"And I never sent the one you received."

They stared at each other, breathless.

It hit her like a punch to the gut.

Oh my God. We were lied to.

Both of us.

But she wasn't ready to accept and forgive. Not yet. She needed time to process that they had been duped. Process that twenty years ago, someone had managed to tear them apart.

She shook her head. "As usual, you don't know what the hell you're talking about."

"Nicole—"

"I don't care. I don't care about twenty voicemails or fake emails or whatever game this is. You walked away after promising me forever. After saying nothing would come between us. And then obviously someone or something did. I'm over it, Tripp."

But was she? Her heart had leaped at the sight of him, and even now, all she wanted to do was lay her mouth over his and remember. But that wasn't going to happen.

She turned on her heel and stormed into her building, heart pounding, throat raw.

Her office was cool, quiet, and blessedly empty. She

closed the door, sank into her chair, and finally let her hands tremble.

Tripp Masterson was back.

And now, they weren't just exes.

They were enemies.

In love. In court. In war.

CHAPTER 3

Tripp Masterson didn't remember leaving Nicole's office building.

One second, he was staring at the back of Nicole's perfectly tailored blazer as she stormed away, her heels echoing like gunshots in his ears. Like bullet holes to his heart. The next, he was gripping the leather steering wheel of his Corvette, heart pounding so hard, it felt like a fist in his chest.

The past had a way of showing up uninvited, and today, it had worn emerald eyes and glossy black hair, and left him shattered during one of the most important trials he'd taken on since returning to the island. A trial he had not originally been the counselor on until the lead lawyer went in for triple-bypass surgery.

He sat behind the wheel for a long moment, staring straight ahead, trying to process what had just happened.

Trying to process the facts he'd learned that still left him stunned.

She thought he had broken up with her. By email.

He'd done no such thing.

His hands tightened on the wheel, knuckles whitening. Fury tangled with confusion in his chest, a knot twenty years in the making. He started the engine and hit the gas. The Corvette roared to life like it knew he needed the speed, needed the release.

What the hell had happened?

She said he never called. That he'd ended their marriage like it was a high school fling. But he *had* called. Again and again. He'd left voicemails. He'd sent messages. He'd begged his parents to let him come back to her.

And then she'd emailed him.

A cold, clinical message with three lines that shattered his heart.

"I've changed my mind. This was a mistake. Please don't contact me again."

He remembered staring at those words on his parents' laptop in a penthouse suite in Greece, sun blazing outside the window, while his insides froze solid.

He'd cried.

Actual tears.

At eighteen.

All their dreams had been shattered by the most venomous text he'd ever read, words so cruel, they cut him to the bone and left him crushed.

And now she stood there in court, confident, brilliant, furious, and swore he had been the one to abandon her?

None of it made sense.

The memory slammed into him.

That morning after the wedding. They'd woken tangled in the sheets of a cheap motel bed, the scent of her skin still on his fingers. At their wedding, she'd worn a veil from the dollar store and no makeup, and she'd never looked more beautiful.

He'd kissed her forehead and promised he'd tell his parents that afternoon. Then he'd walked into his house and everything changed.

His bags were packed.

"Surprise!" his mother had said, too brightly. "We're going to Greece. Your graduation present. Isn't this exciting?"

Before he could say a word, his father had ushered him into a waiting limo. There was no time to argue, no time to fight. They had a plane to catch. They were already late. They'd booked it weeks ago.

Now that he thought back on that morning, they hadn't even questioned him about where he'd been all night.

Had they known?

"I need to call Nicole," he'd said, panicked.

"There'll be time for that later," his mother had said, waving her hand.

There wasn't.

The first day, his cell phone was there, but then that night, it was gone. Claimed it got lost in transit. Every time he tried to use the hotel phone, his parents were suddenly there. He'd asked to go home. They'd refused. Then the week in Greece had turned into a month touring Europe.

By the time he got the email, he was a ghost in her life. And just like that, it was over.

He hit the highway and floored it, the Corvette leaping forward as if it shared his need to outrun everything. The sun burned low over the Gulf, painting the sky in shades of rust and gold, but he barely saw it. His mind was a reel of memories: Nicole's laughter, the night they'd eloped, her crying against his chest when she got her scholarship.

As the reel flickered in his mind, it felt like his chest split wide open, tears stinging his eyes. No, he wasn't that fragile eighteen-year-old anymore, but the ache was still there, sharp and undeniable.

She'd promised him forever.

And then it had ended in a dozen cold words typed onto a screen.

But now? Now he knew something else.

She never got his calls. She never sent that email.

And he sure as hell hadn't sent the one she accused him of.

They'd been played.

But by whom?

He knew.

His parents. Her parents, possibly?

The beach house came into view, a modern architectural gem perched on the dunes, all glass and angles and cold perfection. He hated it. Always had.

He pulled into the circular drive, turned off the engine, and sat for a moment, trying to calm the surge of emotions storming through him.

It didn't work.

He walked up the stone steps and opened the front door without knocking.

"Dustin!" his mother called from the formal sitting room. "You're home early! How lovely."

Not Tripp. Just the name she insisted on using when society was around.

Tripp stepped inside, the scent of white lilies and lemon polish assaulting his senses. Everything was pristine, curated, artificial.

Just like her.

"We're having guests tonight," she continued, breezing toward him in a silk blouse and pearls. "You remember the Pembrokes? Their niece is visiting from Houston. She just passed the bar. Quite accomplished."

Tripp gave a dry laugh. "Let me guess. Blonde, thin, politically conservative, and not a single thought of her own?"

That was the kind of woman his mother liked to introduce him to, and he was tired of thinking she knew what was best for him. Today, he'd had a reminder of what he wanted in a woman. She'd been fighting him in court, and doing a damn good job of being a lawyer.

"Dustin," his mother warned, smoothing imaginary wrinkles from her sleeve. "You're thirty-eight. You've wasted years. It's time to start thinking about your future.

About settling down. About the Masterson name. Your father would expect this of you."

His father was dead, and yet she liked to remind him of what his father expected from him, of how he would run the law firm. All Tripp wanted was to be his own man.

He stared at her. "I did think about my future once. Remember?"

Her expression didn't change. "If you're referring to Nicole Reyes, I hope you've outgrown that foolishness."

No, today proved that whatever time and distance had taken from them, the spark remained—still humming low and steady, like the perfectly tuned engine of a classic car waiting for him to turn the key.

Tripp smiled, but it didn't reach his eyes. "Guess who I saw today. In court."

Her fingers paused on a crystal decanter. "One of your father's old clients?"

"No. Nicole. Reyes. You know. My wife."

Her face went completely still. The ice behind her eyes cracked for just a second.

"I'd hardly call her your wife," she said, too smoothly. "That marriage was annulled. It lasted less than twenty-four hours, because that little witch's family disapproved."

Oh, really? That was more than his mother had ever said before. How did she know that Nicole's family didn't approve?

"She says she never received any of my calls. Says I broke up with her via email. Funny thing is, I never sent her one. But I sure as hell got one from her. And I never responded."

Silence.

"Mom," he said slowly, stepping closer. "Do you know anything about that?"

Her chin snapped up, eyes narrowing in sharp disapproval.

Her mouth twitched. "I barely remember the girl."

"That's a lie. You said her name before I mentioned her."

Her chin lifted higher in defiance. "Excuse me," she replied, crossing her arms like a shield. But her eyes betrayed her, glinting with something between fear and fury. For a moment, her control cracked, the mask slipping enough for him to glimpse the truth beneath.

"I said it's a lie. You remember her. You hated her. You said she was beneath me. You said she was a distraction. You said she was a phase. You called her trash."

His mother flicked her long gray hair over her shoulder like she was on the damn cover of *Town & Country*, not standing there lying through her teeth. He almost applauded the performance. The fake smile, the casual gesture, it was vintage Suzanne Masterson. Polished. Controlled.

And totally full of shit.

He'd seen that move a hundred times.

It was her signature tic.

She always did it when the truth became inconvenient.

"I said what any mother would say. You were too

young. She wasn't right for this family. You had a future to protect."

"So you what?" he snapped. "You took my phone? You sent fake emails from both of us? You destroyed my marriage before it had a chance to breathe?"

She didn't answer.

"I asked you a question."

"I was happy to see it end," she said at last, voice cold and clipped. "You would've thrown away everything for that girl."

That wasn't a lie. He would've moved mountains to keep Nicole smiling. He'd been ready to walk away from Baylor, pack up his dreams, and follow her to Austin. But instead, she'd tossed him aside, swift and merciless, like a hot potato he never saw coming.

"I loved her."

"You were eighteen," she snapped. "It wasn't real."

Tripp's hands curled into fists. "If I learn you sabotaged my marriage, you'll regret the day you ruined my life. I will not take it kindly."

At this point in his life, he could see his mother for exactly the type of woman she was. A cold, selfish, snotty society woman who didn't fraternize with anyone lower than her standing in society. You'd think that type of person had died with the Gilded Age, but you'd be wrong.

"Stop being dramatic. You were eighteen. Ask her parents what happened. It was twenty years ago, and I know nothing except that I was going to protect my son at any cost."

They stared at each other, the air crackling with electricity.

Tripp turned on his heel and walked toward the stairs.

"Dinner is at seven," she called after him like nothing was wrong. That this argument was over, and she'd won. But it was far from over.

"I hear this girl is a beauty."

He didn't answer.

In his old bedroom, still disgustingly untouched like a shrine to the golden boy he used to be, he shut the door, leaned back against it, and exhaled.

His mind was spinning. His heart was wrecked.

He and Nicole hadn't failed.

They'd been tricked.

Most likely by the people who were supposed to protect them.

He sat at his desk and opened his laptop. He had questions. And someone was going to answer them.

If Nicole was back, for good, then he had one shot to make this right.

One chance to rewrite the ending they'd been robbed of.

And he'd be damned if he let anyone take her away from him again.

The only person who might hold the truth was Paige.

He hadn't thought about her in years, but now her name echoed in the back of his mind like a thread he needed to pull. She'd been there that night. She'd known them both, knew what they meant to each other.

He didn't know where she was now. But he'd find her.

Because something had gone terribly wrong, and the past wasn't done with him. Not yet.

If there was even a chance that Paige could help him piece together what really happened, what tore Nicole away from him, he had to take it.

Tripp was done living in the dark. Done swallowing someone else's version of the truth.

He was going to dig up every lie, every hand that pulled the strings, and finally find out who tore his marriage to Nicole apart, and why.

And God help them, there had better be a very good reason.

CHAPTER 4

$\mathcal{N}$icole had thought she'd buried it.

That night.

That chapel.

That boy.

The impossible hope of forever.

She thought it had all been laid to rest in a part of her heart she'd sealed off with steel and silence. But now, the grave had been disturbed.

Robbed actually.

By a man in a navy suit who still knew how to make her heart stutter and her knees weak, even as her brain screamed *don't you dare.*

She stepped through the back door of her parents' house just after sunset. The familiar creak of the hinges greeted her, followed by the scent of simmering onions and warm tortillas. Her mother was at the stove, humming an old love song in Spanish that made Nicole's skin prickle.

Her father, Francisco, sat in his recliner in the den, eyes fixed on a game show, his worn fishing cap tilted low. A can of beer rested on the side table, unopened.

It was like walking into a time capsule.

Same smells.

Same sounds.

Same tension under the surface.

Only now, her two sisters and younger brother were not here to run interference. Nicole slipped off her heels, sighing as her aching feet touched the cool tile.

Though her parents loved one another deeply, her father's health had frightened them and brought her home. All her other siblings were married with children. She'd been the obvious one to take care of them.

"You're late," her mother said without looking up. "Dinner's almost ready."

Nicole dropped her briefcase by the hallway table and leaned against the doorway to the kitchen. "Work ran long. Pre-trial motions."

Her mother glanced at her then, eyes sharp behind her glasses. "That big murder case you mentioned?"

Nicole nodded, brushing a loose strand of dark hair behind her ear. "Yeah. It's going to be high profile."

Her mother stirred the onions, then added a scoop of shredded chicken to the pan. "So… what do you want? The man to get off?"

Nicole smiled faintly. "Just letting you know why I'm late."

She sighed. "I still believe he killed his girlfriend because she was pregnant."

Silence hung for a moment.

Then, softly, she said, "I saw Tripp today."

The spatula froze mid-stir.

In the den, the sound of the TV clicked off.

Nicole didn't move.

Her mother set the spatula down with exaggerated care and turned, her expression unreadable.

"What do you mean?" she asked, too casually. "You saw him where?"

Nicole tilted her head. "He's the defense attorney. On the Reddick case. His law firm is trying to get this man off of murder one."

Her mother blinked. "Oh."

Just *oh*.

Nicole crossed her arms. "That's it? He looked mighty handsome."

"What do you want me to say?" her mother replied, turning back to the stove. "It's been twenty years. People move on. I keep waiting for you to move on. To find another man to love."

She'd dated all through college, always measuring each man against Tripp. Once, she'd even gone so far as to sleep with someone, hoping it might change something inside her, hoping she'd feel different. But afterward—nothing.

Empty. If anything, she'd hated the experience, hated herself for trying to replace what could never be replaced.

"I have moved on," she said. "It's just I don't trust men. They lie."

In the other room, Francisco shifted in his chair but didn't say a word. That was his role, always watching, rarely speaking.

"Not all of us," he said.

"I know, Papa. Momma got the best," she said.

He spoke even less since he had the debilitating heart attack that had him retiring from fishing. He'd even sold his boat and was collecting disability.

Nicole walked farther into the kitchen, her pulse quickening.

How would her mother react to what Tripp had told her today?

"He said something… strange."

As a lawyer, she always enjoyed watching the clients' or witnesses' faces when she asked them a surprise question. There were telltale signs that were easily recognized if you knew what to look for.

Her mother stirred the chicken as if this were just any other evening, just any other conversation. But Nicole knew better. She'd been a lawyer long enough to recognize a witness dodging a trap. To see the tension in her mother's shoulders.

"He said," Nicole continued, "he called me. A lot. After we… after he left."

Her mother didn't respond. Didn't even look up.

Nicole pressed on. "He said he left voicemails. That he never emailed me to end things. That *I* emailed *him*."

Only her mother had access to her email account when she was in school. Only she could have sent that tragic note.

Her mother opened a drawer, pulled out a dish towel, and began wiping down a spotless counter.

Nicole took another step, turning toward her mother. "Did you send that email?"

Her mother's hand stilled. "What email? I'm a house cleaner. What do I know about emails? My kids were the computer gurus, not your father and me. I know nothing of this email."

It was true, but she'd also witnessed her mother checking her brothers' and sisters' emails to make sure they were not being trolled. The woman knew more about computers than she was saying.

Nicole wrapped her arms so tightly across her chest, it felt like she was holding herself together. "You know which email. The one that broke me." The one that gutted her so completely, she could barely get out of bed, drowning in a darkness she wasn't sure she'd ever escape. And the worst part? He'd walked away as if her devastation had been nothing more than collateral damage.

Or at least, she had believed that until today. And even now, she wasn't quite certain what to think.

"I don't." Her mother's voice was soft, slippery. "I don't remember any emails. That was a long time ago."

Nicole's throat tightened. "I remember it."

Thirteen words. Cold. Final. Not a trace of the boy she'd married.

I've changed my mind. This was a mistake. Please don't contact me again.

Her mother still didn't look at her. "Emails get lost. Phones get misplaced. Sometimes people say and do things they regret."

"You didn't answer my question."

Her mother turned then, finally, slowly, her eyes calm but calculating. "Why would I send an email from your account?"

Nicole stared at her. "You tell me."

A beat passed.

"You're my daughter, but I don't get into your email account. That's your business," she said.

That was true now, but had it been back then? Why did this feel wrong? Like she wasn't telling her everything.

Then her mother offered a small, tight smile. "Dinner's ready. Go tell your father."

She was being dismissed. And that made her even more suspicious, twisting the betrayal even tighter in her gut. If they had not sent the emails, who had?

Nicole stood there a moment longer, every muscle in her body humming with something between anger and dread.

Her mother turned back to the stove as if the conversation had never happened.

Nicole walked into the den. Her father hadn't moved.

She leaned against the doorframe and folded her arms. "Did you know he was back?"

"Who?"

He stared at the television, the sound still on mute.

"Tripp Masterson."

Francisco glanced at her. "No."

"Did you know he was the defense attorney on my case?"

"No."

She watched him. "Do you remember what happened? Back then?"

He blinked slowly. "I remember you cried. For days."

And she had. He'd broken her heart and left a scar that still lingered. It was hard to trust someone when you'd been lied to like she had.

"That's all?"

His mouth twitched. "I remember I wanted to kill the boy for breaking your heart."

A typical fatherly response. But did he have something to do with the annulment? It had been delivered to the house by someone from Tripp's father's law firm. All she'd had to do was sign.

Nicole let out a dry laugh. "I thought he left me. Just walked away. But now... I don't know. Something's not right."

Francisco didn't respond. Instead, he stared at the television screen that he'd muted.

Nicole looked back toward the kitchen.

"She's hiding something."

Her father took a sip of his beer, which was now open. "She always was better at keeping secrets than I was. Still is."

Was she keeping secrets from Nicole about Tripp?

"I'm going to find out the truth," she said.

"What good will that do? Leave the past in the past," her father said, glancing up from the television, his expression tight and drawn.

Nicole's chest tightened. "Did you want us to end?"

Francisco didn't answer right away. Then: "I wanted you to be happy. I didn't think he could give you that. You're my beautiful daughter, and I want the best for you. Even after twenty years, I still want the best for you."

Everyone assumed that they couldn't be happy. Even her friend Paige had doubted their marriage would last.

Nicole swallowed hard. "Maybe he could've made me happy."

Her father didn't look at her. "Doubtful. What took him so long to return to the island?"

"Don't know. But he's my opponent in court. He's my enemy until I put his man away," she said. "And his family is still in control of him. He's working at his father's law firm."

Why she'd been surprised, she didn't know. But he'd always said he didn't want to follow in his father's foot-steps. That he wanted his own firm.

Francisco gave her a look. "So was I the day I asked your mother to marry me. Her father threatened to shoot me."

Nicole shook her head, a bitter smile on her lips. "That's not the same."

Francisco raised an eyebrow. "It's not that different."

Nicole didn't answer. She pushed away from the doorframe and walked slowly back to her room.

She sat on the edge of her childhood bed, the same one with the quilt her abuela had made, the same bookshelf full of old paperbacks and forgotten notebooks, and stared at the wall.

Her mother had lied.

Not outright. Not with words. But in that way, women like her mother always did with half-smiles and carefully placed silences. Tonight, Nicole had set the stage for uncovering the truth. Her mother might sense she was probing, testing the edges, but soon, subtlety would no longer be enough. She was done living with shadows. She would find out who had torn them apart, and why, even if it broke her all over again.

And now, for the first time in two decades, Nicole felt the terrible, shifting weight of doubt.

What if Tripp hadn't separated them?

What if it had been the people who claimed to love them both?

Her heart twisted, unsure of what to believe. Her memory clashed with her logic, her instinct with her resentment.

She reached for her phone, hesitated, then opened her email.

There it was. Still saved. A scar she'd never deleted.

I've changed my mind. This was a mistake. Please don't contact me again.

No greeting. No emotion. No closure. Nothing like the Tripp who had married her and loved her.

No mention of the wedding.

She stared at it for a long time.

Then, for the first time in twenty years, she hit reply. Would he answer? Did he still have the same email address?

She didn't type anything. Just stared at the blinking cursor.

Quickly, she typed. She needed to make this clear. She had to try.

Someone is lying.

A few minutes later, she got a response.

I know, he wrote. *I'm going to find out who. And it wasn't me. Meet me at Charlie's for dinner tomorrow night.*

No. Time to let the past be the past.

They were on opposite sides of a trial that would determine a man's life. She would not be meeting with him. And even if she could, she needed time to accept this new reality.

It wasn't Tripp's fault their marriage was annulled. But who had done this to them?

CHAPTER 5

Tripp Masterson stared at the monitor long after everyone else in the office had gone home. His fingers hovered over the keyboard, motionless, his body present but his mind anchored twenty years in the past.

The past, it seemed, had just come roaring back with emerald eyes and black-as-night hair, wrapped in courtroom steel.

Nicole Reyes.

He hadn't expected to see her again, especially not as opposing counsel in the biggest murder trial this town had seen in a decade.

And now, everything he'd buried, everything he thought he'd moved past, was clawing to the surface with a vengeance.

The hurt.

The rage.

The love.

The truth, whatever it was, had never been told.

He swallowed hard and finally typed her name: Paige McLane.

She was the only one who'd known about the elopement that night. The only one who might still have the missing piece of the story. If anyone remembered the truth about that night, before the lies, the annulment, and the wreckage, it would be Paige.

To hell with legal databases. He wasn't looking for a criminal record, just a lifeline.

The firm's system spat out a location: Fort Collins, Colorado. No criminal charges. Just an address, and, luckily, a still-active number.

He dialed.

One ring.

Two.

"This is Paige."

He closed his eyes, and for a second, the years fell away. Her voice still had the same easy warmth it always did. Sarcasm tucked under sincerity.

"Are you still as beautiful as you were twenty years ago?"

Silence.

"Who is this?"

He chuckled. "You don't recognize my voice? I'm offended."

Another pause.

"Tripp?"

"It's me, darling, with a lot of time and baggage etched

on my face," he said, thinking the last time he'd seen her, they had all been so young – high school graduation. "Older, grayer, but still reasonably charming."

She let out a low, disbelieving laugh. "Wow. Tripp Masterson. Who died?"

"No one. Not yet."

"You married?"

"Divorced," he said. "How about you?"

"Nope. I'm still happily single. I love my life here in Colorado," she said. "Though I may come home soon. Where are you living?"

After years in Dallas, he'd come home only after his father's death. It wasn't the way he'd imagined returning, but someone had to keep the family law firm afloat, and his mother had made it clear she expected it to be him. Still, nothing had prepared him for Nicole. Seeing her again had been the one thing he hadn't planned for.

"After my father passed, I moved back to the island, and I'm running the law firm now," he said, knowing that as angry as he'd been at his father for the annulment, he still missed him.

"Any kids?" she asked.

"Nope," he said. "No, my second marriage didn't last long enough to have kids."

Come to think of it, neither of his marriages lasted long.

There was silence on the phone. "It's great to hear your voice, but it must be serious for you to call me out of the blue like this. You've had my number for twenty years."

"I've had a lot of things for twenty years. Regret. Rage. Confusion," he said with a sigh. "I saw Nicole today."

She sobered. "Nicole?"

"Nicole."

Another pause, longer this time.

"You saw her?"

"We're opposing counsel in a murder trial," he said.

That got a full-throated laugh out of her. "You're kidding. The two of you fighting in court after all this time. It's like the universe is saying you have unfinished business between the two of you. And that must be the reason for your call."

"I need answers. Answers from twenty years ago."

"It's taken you twenty years to call and ask me what happened that night. Twenty fucking years. I kept waiting for your call to ask me what happened, but nothing. Absolutely nothing."

He'd tried to reach her, but stranded in a foreign country without his phone, it was impossible. By the time he made it back, the damage was done. The marriage was over, the relationship shattered—and all he could do was gather the jagged pieces of his life and force himself to keep moving.

"What can I say? I was young, stupid, and so in love with Nicole that I couldn't believe she ended our marriage before it even had a chance to begin. I went from Europe to college. It took me months to get over her, and I think I've hated her for the last twenty years."

"You two were so in love. I had such high hopes for you," she said. "She told me that you broke it off. Did you?"

"No, she said the same thing to me outside of the courtroom." He smiled faintly. "Today was surreal. But also... maddening. She thinks I abandoned her. That I walked away. She brought up some email, one I supposedly sent. I never did."

Silence.

He pressed his palm to his eyes. "I thought she changed her mind. I thought she... I don't know. Regretted marrying me. She emailed me saying it was a mistake. And then, nothing. She ghosted me. Never answered my calls. Never wrote. Nothing."

"She told me the same thing," Paige said softly. "That you broke it off with her. That you wanted your freedom. That your parents pressured you and you went along with it."

"That's not what happened."

"I know," Paige whispered. "At least, I suspected something wasn't right. But, what good is digging up all of this now?"

Tripp sat back, heart pounding. "I need closure. To understand what happened so I don't repeat the same mistake. Tell me. Please. What do you remember?"

She was quiet for a long moment.

"My mom... she figured it out. She always had a sixth sense when something was going on. You two were too lovesick to hide anything, especially from our mothers."

The last night, at the party, he'd seen Paige's mother

watching them. If he had to do it over again, he'd be much better at sneaking off.

"I didn't tell you where we were going."

"I didn't need to know the address." There was a heavy sigh. "My mother insisted I tell your mother what you and Nicole were doing. Somehow my mother figured out that something was up. So about an hour after you left, I had to tell your mother and father where the two of you had gone. Thank goodness you didn't tell me the name of the chapel, or they would have put toothpicks under my nails to get me to talk. I didn't dare try to reach you, because they were watching me very carefully. My mother had eyes like an eagle hawk in the front and back of her head."

Reaching up, he rubbed his temple, feeling his headache from what she was telling him. So his parents had known they were eloping and had been unable to stop them. "What about Nicole's parents? Were they there?"

"No, but your mother was looking up their address. I think she thought they were in on the wedding. That they had a reception planned or something, so she wanted to go and stop the partying."

Nicole's parents were rather sedate and would have been home watching television or in bed due to how early her father rose each morning.

"That's all I know. I don't know what happened after your parents left the country club in such a ditter. Your mother was crying," she said. "And your father just kept shaking his head."

The memories swam before his eyes, and he closed

them against the pain. "It was a beautiful ceremony. We told the preacher she was pregnant, and he married us right away. Afterward, we went to the Salt Bay Inn and spent the night."

The vision of her long, dark hair curling down her back, the satin white nightgown clinging to her curves, had him almost moaning. They'd been so in love, and that night, he almost wished they had created a baby. At least then, maybe they would still be together.

"What happened when you told your parents?"

He ran a hand over his face. "They ambushed me. Bags packed. Private jet waiting. I didn't even have time to grab my phone charger."

"I never saw Nicole again after that night," Paige said. "She vanished. A week later, I heard she was already in Austin for early registration. I assumed you'd worked it out privately. But then... nothing. I heard rumors about an annulment, but no one ever talked about it."

Her parents had shipped her off early too. But why? What excuse had they given? Deep down, he suspected it wasn't about her at all; it was about him. About making sure their precious daughter never wasted another second on the boy they thought wasn't good enough.

"I didn't work anything out," Tripp said, voice thick with emotion. "They took me to Europe and cut off my world. When we got back, Dad handed me the annulment papers and said Nicole had already signed. I didn't question it. I was too angry, too hurt."

"Did you call her?"

God, how he'd called her. Over and over, but she never picked up. Had her mother blocked his number? Surely, someone could have told her he was trying. Yet when he lost his phone, every contact vanished—and with it, any chance of reaching the people who might have bridged the gap between them. "I tried. Dozens of messages. No response."

"She said you never called."

That wasn't true. And the thought of her carrying that lie in her heart—believing it of him—shattered him, breaking something so deep inside he wasn't sure it could ever be put back together.

"I know. Which makes me wonder... did she even get my messages? Or was someone intercepting everything?"

Paige didn't speak right away. Then she said, "You think someone faked the emails?"

"Don't you?"

"Your parents or hers," she said flatly. "Hell, maybe both. We were all telling her to wait. Telling her that if it was meant to be, it would survive a few months apart. Maybe someone thought they were helping her."

"Helping?" Tripp spat. "By burning down everything we were building?"

"She was seventeen, Tripp."

"And I was eighteen. And we were in love."

And everyone and everything had been against them. It had felt like the whole world was against them, every voice, every circumstance, every force conspiring to pull them apart.

Paige's voice softened. "I believe you. I always did."

He leaned forward, elbows on the desk, head in his hands. "I saw her today and... it wrecked me. She's still so damn beautiful. Still brilliant. Still... her."

How could he face her every day? It was going to be difficult.

"You're not over her."

He'd lied to himself all these years, telling himself that he was over her. That it was just a young man's foolish mistake, and then he'd seen her. All five-foot-four, one-hundred-ten-pounds, dripping wet.

But he wasn't ready to admit to anyone that with one look, all those feelings came rushing back.

There was a long silence between them, heavy with old memories and unspoken regret.

Finally, Paige said, "So what do you want from me?"

"I need to know everything you remember. Everyone who could've had a hand in it. Every odd conversation. Every look. Every overheard comment."

"I'll think. I'll go through my old journals."

"You kept journals?"

"Of course. I was seventeen. I wrote down every tragic romance event. And I'll be honest with you, Tripp... I don't think you're going to like what you find."

It was a risk he was willing to take. Maybe he'd learn that Nicole did indeed end the relationship, but he didn't think so.

"I already don't. I couldn't help but think what if? What if we'd stayed together? What if we had a family by now?

What if we had gone to law school together, taken the bar together? It was our dream. And now here we are, both of us lawyers, neither one of us married, and I find it very hard to trust women."

Maybe they were both still trapped in the past, still struggling to climb out from under the weight of what had happened.

"What do you want to do, Trippy?"

It was a name she'd called him all through school, and he hated it. And she knew he did.

"I want to learn the truth. I have to know if she was the one who ended our relationship or if someone else spoke for her. But who could that be?"

"Oh, her mother, your mother, her father, your father, or even one of her friends. We were all telling her that if it was meant to be, you guys would last without being married. Without going to school together."

It was true. Their families did not approve, and even some of her girlfriends thought they needed to wait. But they wanted to be together.

"Does Nicole know that you're digging up the past?"

"Kind of," he said. "She'd saved the old email I supposedly sent and responded to it. I received it tonight. I *did not* write that email. She told me someone is lying. I agreed with her and asked her out to dinner. She turned me down."

When she turned him down, it hit like a brutal gut punch, stealing his breath. They were supposed to keep their distance, opposing counsel locked in a trial, nothing more. But the truth was, once this case ended, Nicole might need more than courtroom walls to hold him back. She might need a restraining order.

"I would think since you're on opposing teams, it would be unethical for the two of you to fraternize at all. It's a murder trial, and the man's life is on the line."

He'd thought about that, but as long as they didn't talk about the trial, they should be all right. And yet it didn't look good at all. But he wanted to learn the truth.

"We'll have to be careful, but so far, she's turned me down. When I present her with evidence, I'm hoping she'll agree. So now, I have to find evidence that someone sent emails in our names. This was not what we wanted, and the only people who I feel certain wanted to break us up were our parents."

Paige sighed. "Yeah, her mother wanted her to concentrate on school. And your mother just hated her family because they were white trash and not rich like your family."

It was true. As much as he hated it, his mother was one dramatic society diva.

Another pause.

"I'm coming back to Mustang Island," Paige said suddenly. "I need to see you two. Witness the explosion that will soon be coming."

He hadn't seen this coming. Still, he remembered how close Nicole and Paige had once been, inseparable, really. Maybe seeing each other again would be good for them, a chance to bridge the years that had slipped by.

"What?"

"I need to be there for this. For her. For you. For whatever the hell this is."

"You'd do that?"

"I owe it to both of you. And I want to see the truth come out."

He closed his eyes again, his throat tightening.

"I never stopped loving her," he admitted. "And I think... I think she didn't stop loving me either."

"Then fight for her," Paige said. "But be careful. You're in court together. Don't give anyone a reason to call a mistrial."

The words slid over him with an ease that unsettled him, as if they belonged to them, tailored perfectly to fit the chaos of what he and Nicole were.

He nodded, though she couldn't see it.

"I'll be careful," he promised. "But I'm not backing down."

"Then I'll see you soon, Tripp Masterson."

He hung up slowly. For the first time in twenty years, the fog was starting to lift.

He didn't have all the answers yet.

But he had a direction. And a reason.

Nicole hadn't walked away. Neither had he.

They'd been shoved.

And now, after all this time, he was finally going to find out by whom. Time to learn who had ended their happily ever after before it had a chance to begin.

CHAPTER 6

The Salt & Vine wine bar was already humming with quiet laughter and live acoustic guitar when Nicole walked in. Nestled between a small art gallery and a candle shop on the side street, it was the kind of place where the lighting hugged you gently, and the air smelled of oak barrels, aged Merlot, and something altogether nostalgic.

She spotted her girls in their usual booth by the window. The low, leather cushions looked the same, and for a beat, she could go back to being seventeen again. Jennifer's blonde hair was pulled up in a carefree bun; Amanda's eyes glistened with something brave; Crystal, glowing, hand gently resting on her belly. And there, tucked to the side, was a new face in the group, Paige.

Her breath caught. Paige, in the flesh, beautiful and vibrant, her presence like a spark that made everything in the room shift.

Nicole ran to her friend's side. Twenty long years lay between them, and while she was still the most gorgeous girl on the island, Nicole needed to hug her good friend. Suddenly, she felt fifteen again, heart pounding, palms sweating as they sneaked off to search for boys.

"I'm so happy you're here," she said. "It's been way too long. How long are you visiting?"

"Only for a few weeks, and then I have to return."

"Ladies!" she announced, voice louder than she meant. The music softened in recognition as the women turned, smiles blooming like wildflowers.

They rose, laughter threading through them, a five-way hug that felt older and firmer than the last time they'd done this. Nicole felt Paige's arms tighten around her as though, together, they carried two decades of shared history forward in a heartbeat.

Paige squeezed into the booth beside Nicole, and immediately, the space felt right.

Jennifer was first to get an order in: "Prosecco to start, darling?" She looked from Nicole to Paige with a mischievous grin. "And whatever the house red is, bring that to me. We need to celebrate tonight, the old group being back together."

Crystal, always refined, chose water. "Something soft and comforting," she said, rubbing her own belly gently. "This little one is too young to drink."

Two years ago, Crystal had found her happily ever after with a man here on the island. Three years ago, Jennifer had found love for the second time with a boy she'd dated one summer. Amanda was reeling from a divorce. Nicole had returned to the Island, and now Paige was here, as well.

Amanda sat on the edge of the group, eyes fierce and sad, nodded to the bartender, saying quietly, "Whatever helps me forget the world exists for fifteen minutes. Surprise me."

Nicole watched this scene, the perfume-light laughter, the strength flickering in Amanda's expression, the way Paige's return shifted something in the air. She grabbed the wine list, thumb lingering.

"What brought you home?" Nicole asked, unable to mask the edge in her voice. She needed to know why Paige had shown up so suddenly, so unannounced.

"Tripp called me," Paige said quietly. "He wanted to ask about the night you two got married."

Nicole froze, her breath catching. Stunned, she stared at her friend. *What did she know?* And more importantly, *what had Tripp told her?*

Fear coiled in Nicole's chest as she wondered what Paige had told him. Even now, just hearing his name sent Nicole's heart racing. Paige had come back, was it because she cared, or because no one else could patch the holes the past had torn open? And now here they were: five women, four stories of heartbreak, and one wildcard returning to upend everything.

Nicole finally ordered a Malbec, its deep red color promising comfort, complexity, and the courage to speak truths.

The wine arrived, and glasses clinked. Paige's smooth voice cut through the ambient music.

"So this is happening, courtroom showdowns with Nicole Reyes," she said, raising her glass to Nicole. "The city's newest prosecutor."

"Against who?" Jennifer asked.

"Tripp," Paige replied. "They're facing off in court."

Nicole braced herself, letting out a wry smile. "Yes. Opposing counsel. It was like the universe decided: unfinished business."

"Exactly," Paige said. "About time."

"Can we laugh about it?" Jennifer asked, twirling her glass. "Because if not, I might fall into my chair and cry all over again."

"I don't know what happened, but it gutted all of us to learn that your marriage had been annulled," Amanda said. "Tell us."

"We eloped the night after graduation and were married in a beautiful little chapel. We spent the night at the inn, and then the next thing I know, I'm receiving an email from him saying he wants to party while he's at college. Please don't contact him again."

Jennifer's brow drew together. "That doesn't sound like Tripp."

"No, he was crazy about you," Crystal said.

"I always thought that you and he would live happily ever after. I guess that's something I don't believe in any longer," Amanda said with a sigh.

"So what happened?" Jennifer asked. "Was it from his

email?"

"Oh yes," she said with a sigh. "His father drew up an annulment. A month after we were married, the marriage was no more. The only thing I lost was my virginity and my trust in men."

Even speaking of that time still cut deep, the ache as sharp as ever. Would she ever heal from it, or was she destined to carry the wound forever?

Paige sighed. "To be fair, Tripp's family met him at the door the next morning and whisked him off to Europe for the summer."

"How do you know that?" Nicole asked, knowing her family and his had once been friends.

"He told me," she said. "This is why the two of you need to talk."

"We're opposing counsel," Nicole reminded her.

Paige shook her head. "You need to talk."

"Not now. Regardless, I never heard from him again," Nicole said, her heart aching at the memory of how she just wanted to speak to him. To confirm that the annulment was what he wanted. And yet her heart called her ten times a fool for even considering talking to him again.

"Wow, and you kept the annulment a secret. Why is it coming out now?" Crystal asked.

"Because we're both back in town and dueling in court. He's on one side of the courtroom, and I'm on the other. And for the first time in twenty years, we actually spoke."

There was silence as they emptied a bottle of red wine.

Amanda managed a dry laugh. "I tried to call my husband five times today. Nothing."

Paige reached over and nestled a hand on Amanda's. "You're not alone. We've got your back. I know it's hard, but let him go."

Nicole watched Amanda's shoulders shift, hope nudging through her sorrow. Could something like this have happened to her and Tripp if they'd stayed together? She would never know.

Crystal cleared her throat. "Okay, but we still need to dish about Paige. Are you really here for Nicole or for a summer fling?"

Paige's eyes lit up. "I came for Nicole, because I'm hoping she and Tripp will learn the truth. I want to help. But if sparks fly, I won't stop them. Promise."

Nicole's breath caught. She looked into Paige's warm gray eyes, and something quiet bloomed between them.

They talked. They drank. They reminisced. Light giggles underlined stories from prom nights and secret crushes; their hands reached for food off the shared charcuterie board, cheese, crusty bread, marinated olives, and strawberries.

Jennifer looked at Nicole and said gently, "I used to think you loved Tripp more than you loved us."

Nicole swallowed a bite of brie. "I loved him...and I was terrified of what I'd do if he walked away. And now, I know how I'd react. I'd be fine. I'd survive. But that first year of college was rough."

Silence.

Nicole's lips trembled.

Paige leaned in close. "I'm sorry about the past. But I had to come home, Nicole. And I'm here to help, whatever that looks like."

Nicole blinked back tears. "Thank you...especially tonight."

Their laughter softened as tears seeped in. Amanda's gaze broke away for a moment.

"Well," Amanda said softly, "I found out a few days ago that Joe, my husband, has been living a double life for years. With a man. That's his reason for a divorce. My husband is gay."

The table went still.

"I never dreamed that the divorce could get worse, but now I know the truth. Now, I know why he won't go to counseling. Now I understand why he lost interest in sex. Now I know that there was nothing I could do to keep him."

Paige slipped her arm around Amanda's shoulders. "Shocking. So much for twenty years of marriage."

Amanda swallowed. "I don't know who I am anymore. I've always been a wife and mother. Now I'm just a mother of five kids who have all grown up and moved away except for Brent. He's the last chick at home.. No one needs me anymore."

"We need you," Crystal said, rubbing her own rounded belly. "Remember this is baby number two, and I still have trouble when they get sick. You're the calming force that helps me see that this is just part of life and I'm not going to kill them."

Nicole giggled. "I'd be terrified."

"I was," Crystal said.

Jennifer grabbed Amanda's hand. "Honey, you write your own second act. We're all here to cheer you on. Look at me. My second act is so much better than the first."

The women leaned into each other, a cocoon of empathy and shared vulnerability. There were tears, confessions, and hugs as they huddled. Nicole had never felt closer to these women than she did just now.

Nicole caught Paige's eye; it had been so long. No words were needed, just a breath passed between them.

Paige whispered, "Want me to go with you tomorrow to the courthouse? Just...supporting you in the back."

Tomorrow was the first day of the trial. Tomorrow was the day she would face her nemesis and, oh, how she wanted to beat him.

Nicole nodded, feeling nervous about sparring with Tripp. "That'd mean everything."

They lifted their glasses.

"To the women who write their own stories," Jennifer toasted.

"To love we once thought lost," Crystal added.

"To family by choice," Amanda said.

Nicole held Paige's gaze, the wine warm in her belly, the past dissolving in the glow of this moment.

For the first time in years, she felt ready to believe that love didn't just end. Sometimes it just needed the right room, the right voices, and a glass of wine to come home again.

"To being strong and not needing a man to make our life happy. We make our own happiness," Paige said.

"To beating Tripp in court," she said.

"Cheers," they all cried.

Maybe it was vindictive, but twenty years of believing he'd betrayed her didn't just vanish overnight. It would take time and answers before she could accept that they'd both been deceived.

Until the trial was over, the courtroom would be the only place their voices touched—each word laced with everything they couldn't say.

CHAPTER 7

The courtroom smelled like old wood, tempered by the low hum of anticipation, a breath the room already held before everything began. Silver beams of morning filtered through stained-glass windows, illuminating specks of dust drifting in still air. Nicole Reyes stood at the prosecution's table, fingertips brushing the polished surface, while in the corner of her mind, Bianca Laurent's face glowed, alive and hopeful, against everything that had taken her away.

Nicole inhaled slowly, grounding herself. Today was more than just another case. It was therapy, reckoning, and a retribution of her own.

Twenty years ago, that could have been me.

She pressed her hands flat, and the belief echoed underneath her skin. If she'd gotten pregnant that night, would Tripp have reacted the way she believed Bianca's boyfriend had? The man came from a wealthy family, and they'd done everything they could to make it appear that Bianca had more than one man in her life.

But it had all been lies. Nicole had found no one. Only some disturbing texts from the man she believed killed her, upset that she had gotten pregnant. Begging her to get an abortion. More texts from the killer's mother. Upset that she'd trapped her son.

It seemed like an echo from her past. But she wasn't going to let them win. Nicole would defend this girl's life like it was her own.

Across the aisle sat Dustin "Tripp" Masterson, calm. Precise. Controlled. He adjusted his cufflinks the way he used to brush wisps of hair from her shoulder. The steel in his eyes she recognized from when he played high school football. He was here to win, but so was she.

They were no longer lovers. They were adversaries. And yet...the memories of their younger lives filled her. She could have been Bianca. He could have been Reddick.

Nicole squared her shoulders. This trial belonged to Bianca now. But ten thousand miles of emotion made every breath personal.

"State of Texas versus Derrick Reddick," the bailiff announced, voice rolling across polished benches. "All rise."

The courtroom exhaled as Judge Carlton Price entered, robes swaying, aura commanding. He surveyed everyone with calm authority.

"Be seated," he said simply. His voice was quiet but full,

homely, firm. "We convene the trial of *State v. Reddick*. Counsel, please state your appearances."

Nicole inhaled, lifted her chin. She would win this trial.

Nicole rose then. "Nicole Reyes, for the prosecution."

Their eyes met, an electric collision. Lightning and ice. Everything that had been buried: pain, regret, resentment, past love. It was all right there.

The words tasted like iron and hope.

Tripp stood across the aisle.

"Dustin Masterson, Defense."

Lightning lanced her chest. She blinked, pushing away memories.

No, she whispered in her mind. *This is not about us. This is about Bianca.*

Jennifer and Paige, her friends in the gallery, were watching. She gave them a subtle nod.

She began voir dire with a professional edge, crisp, probing.

"Ladies and gentlemen, do any of you know the defendant or the victim, Bianca Laurent? Have you read media accounts?"

Each juror offered a nod or shake of the head. Their expressions were open, eyes earnest, maybe even anxious.

She explained herself:

"Bianca Laurent wasn't just a victim. She was a law student, someone once full of promise. She was a plaintiff; yesterday, you could have been her."

She glimpsed Tripp's gaze flicker, sharp. Skewed. He

watched her, questioning whether this was case preparation or confession.

She inhaled again. In the prosecution's binder rested Bianca's acceptance letter to law school—Nicole's dream, too, once. She gently fingered it, breathing courage.

When it was time, Nicole's voice rose before the jury.

"Members of the jury, Bianca Laurent was bright, courageous, and full of dreams, dreams much like some of yours. She anticipated law school; she was planning a life she believed in."

She paused, heart hammering.

"And yet, her life ended. Not by accident, but by a man she trusted."

Her voice caught on "trusted."

"He was a local man from a good family. I'm going to prove he threatened her. Lied. Shot her. Abandoned the life growing inside her. The life together they created. Why? Because Bianca wasn't in the same social sphere as Mr. Reddick. And his family disapproved."

Her words tumbled with force, conviction, and pain.

"It wasn't just her and the baby's lives stolen, it was her future. And the promise of justice depends on you. You will be asked to listen, to decide who killed Bianca."

She finished, breath steady. No tears. It was the hardest opening she'd ever delivered, because she and the victim had so much in common.

This could've been me.

Bianca was her reflection in a mirror she never asked to

look into, but didn't want to look away from either. And she'd do everything she could to bring her killer to justice.

As she sat at the desk, she watched Tripp put his notes down, remembering that night they'd consummated their wedding vows. Her heart thudded in her chest, and she willed the pain away. This was no place for those memories.

Tripp stood, collected himself, and his voice filled the courtroom with stillness.

"Ladies and gentlemen, stories are powerful. They can guide us or mislead us."

He paused.

"My client...loved Bianca. Not just like any man, but because he believed in her. His grief that night shattered him."

He referenced her wounds, but not his thesis on the killer.

"I will show you gaps, inconsistencies... reason to doubt the narrative. This is a man wrongly accused of murdering the woman he loved. Of the child he was excited about. This story will not have the conclusion you expect. My client has lost so much, and I will exonerate him."

She felt something unsheathe inside her, breaking. Because his words were persuasive, and they touched places only she thought were hers.

He sank down, and the judge looked at her.

Her pulse quickened. This was more than strategy; it

was personal. Time to prove herself. Time to win. And time to make Tripp lose—no matter how much it hurt.

"The prosecution would like to call our first witness, Officer Reynolds," she said.

The policeman walked up to the podium, and she glanced down at her notes one final time.

Officer Reynolds, the first to arrive at the murder scene.

After the bailiff swore him in, she walked up to the podium. At first, they talked about how long he'd been with the island's police force. Once she'd established he was a seasoned veteran, she started to ask her questions.

"When did you receive the call?"

"It was about ten thirty at night, when Ms. Laurent's neighbor called to say she'd heard a gunshot. The woman was frightened and said that she knew Miss Laurent and her boyfriend had been arguing a lot. She was afraid something had happened."

"How long did it take you to arrive on scene?"

"About five minutes," he said.

"What kind of call did dispatch say this was?"

"Possible domestic violence, with shots fired," he said.

Nicole felt tears behind her eyelids. But she stayed poised.

"When you arrived, what did you find?"

"When she didn't answer the door, I went around back and saw a body through a window, lying on the floor unconscious. Blood pooled from the back of her head and also from a gunshot to her chest," he said. "Immediately, I called for backup and also an ambulance. Then I entered the house and found that she was deceased."

She asked her expert to bring up photos. One: Bianca's class yearbook, laughing, dreams in her eyes.

When that image filled the screen, Nicole's vision tunneled.

It hurt because she knew that smile.

Tripp caught it too, fleeting recognition in his eyes: *her* smile.

Nicole swallowed.

"Do you recognize this woman?"

"Yes, that's Bianca Laurent," he said.

"Was she the dead person on the floor?"

"Yes," he said.

She paused, letting the jury feel the gravity.

A calmness came over her as she questioned the witness, and she felt confident that Reddick had killed her victim.

When she thought she was done, she walked toward her desk. "Your witness."

Tripp stood and walked to the podium. "Thanks for coming in today, Officer. You said when you arrived, the victim was already deceased. Did anyone prevent you from searching other areas of the house?"

The officer blinked. "We were focused on securing the scene until forensics arrived. That's protocol."

Tripp nodded. "Did you secure the house?"

"Yes, sir. Officer Hill and I checked the rest of the house and secured it."

Tripp questioned the officer quietly: "You found the body in the living room. But the back door, left ajar?"

The officer fumbled.

"Odd, right?"

Nicole's stomach dropped. The crime scene was unraveling even within minutes.

She watched Tripp's pen hover over evidence charts.

"Did you find a murder weapon?"

"No, sir," he replied.

"No further questions, your honor," he said and returned to his chair.

"Call your next witness," the judge said.

"The prosecution calls Detective Larry Spencer," Nicole said, her voice steady as she rose.

The detective took the stand, the oath echoing in the quiet chamber. Nicole approached the podium, heels clicking softly against the polished wood. For the first few minutes, she walked the jury through his credentials—twenty-five years on the force, homicide division veteran, certified in evidence collection. Solid. Reliable. Exactly what they needed to hear. She saw a few jurors nodding faintly, as though reassured this man knew his work.

"Detective, tell us what you observed when you arrived at the scene."

"The deceased was lying on her side," Spencer said, his voice even, practiced. "She appeared to be curled in on herself, as if trying to protect her stomach."

Nicole let the silence linger, watching the jurors' eyes shift down to their notepads. *Good. Let them picture it. Let them feel the vulnerability of a woman shielding her unborn child.*

"Was a murder weapon recovered at the scene?"

"No, ma'am. The scene was clean. However, under forensic lighting, we located fibers and two strands of hair."

"Whose hair did you find?"

"One strand matched the victim. The other matched Mr. Reddick."

A sharp rustle went through the jury box, one juror biting her lip, another jotting down furiously. Nicole kept her expression neutral. Inside, she allowed herself one small flicker of satisfaction.

"Did you examine the victim's phone?"

"Yes. We recovered several text messages between Mr. Reddick and the victim regarding her pregnancy."

"The prosecution moves to admit Exhibit One," Nicole said, lifting the transcript.

The judge nodded, and the texts flashed on the courtroom screen. Nicole's gaze stayed on the jury, watching their faces as the words scrolled:

Reddick: *We used condoms. That baby can't be mine.*

Laurent: *Do you think I'm sleeping with anyone else?*

Reddick: *Well, it's not my baby.*

Laurent: *Condoms break. You remember the night one tore. This baby is yours, and I'm upset you'd doubt me.*

Reddick: *This isn't a good time to have a baby. Let's consider an abortion.*

Laurent: *I'm not getting an abortion. If you don't want me and the baby, that's fine.*

Nicole stayed still, letting the words hang in the air. *Better the jury sees his direct words than hear them from me.*

"After reviewing those texts and finding the hair at the scene, what was your next step?"

"We obtained a warrant to search Mr. Reddick's apartment."

"What did you find?"

"We recovered a firearm from his closet."

Later, she had a firearms expert who would give testimony on the gun.

"Were Mr. Reddick's prints on the gun?"

"No. It had been wiped, but there was no question—it was the weapon."

Nicole then guided him through the details: forensic report requests, gunshot residue, and DNA evidence consistent with Reddick's.

A ripple of unease moved through the gallery. Nicole gave a curt nod. "Thank you, Detective. No further questions, Your Honor."

She glanced across the aisle, catching Tripp's steady gaze. *Your move.* "Your witness."

Tripp rose slowly, buttoning his jacket, every movement deliberate. A few jurors leaned forward, curious, expectant. He approached the podium with calm authority.

"Detective, were there other messages between my client and Miss Laurent?"

"Yes."

"After that argument, did they reconcile?"

"The last message was from Mr. Reddick. He said he was coming over so they could talk about the baby."

"And what else did he say?"

"He told her he loved her."

A murmur rippled through the room. One juror glanced sideways at another, eyebrows raised. Nicole's stomach clenched. *Damn it.* She knew about that message. Hoped it would stay buried. Now it was front and center.

"Were there any messages from other men?" Tripp asked. His tone was smooth, deceptively casual.

Nicole shot to her feet. "Objection, Your Honor. The officer is not qualified to speculate."

"Sustained," the judge said evenly, though Nicole caught the faint narrowing of his eyes. He knew what Tripp was doing, planting the seed without needing the answer.

But Spencer continued. "No. Only from Mr. Reddick's mother."

Nicole braced herself.

"What did she say?"

"She accused Miss Laurent of trapping her son, said the baby would never be accepted, and suggested she get an abortion."

"And Miss Laurent's reply?"

Spencer chuckled. "She told her to go fuck herself."

The courtroom erupted in laughter, the sound rolling through the gallery. Even a couple of jurors cracked reluctant smiles. Nicole's jaw tightened.

This wasn't a comedy routine. It was a murder trial.

"And how did Mrs. Reddick respond?"

"She called Miss Laurent white trash and accused her of chasing their money."

"And Miss Laurent's reply?"

"She didn't respond. Phone records obtained by a warrant show that she blocked his mother's number after that."

"No further questions, Your Honor." Tripp returned to his seat, expression carefully neutral.

Nicole sat back, forcing her breathing to remain even. Inside, frustration burned. *He managed to plant the idea of other lovers in the jurors' minds without evidence. And worse, he softened them with laughter. Damn him. He is good at this.*

Nicole's eyes flicked toward him again, a warning. He met it with a flicker of regret. How strange that she could still understand his body language.

"We'll adjourn for the day and resume at nine a.m. I would like to remind the jury that you are not permitted to discuss this case with anyone."

Nicole exhaled, feeling utterly exhausted by the day's trial.

"Good job, counselor," Craig said. "I'm going to make some calls and then I'm going home."

"See you in the morning," she said, noticing that her friends had slipped out. She'd told them she couldn't speak to them in the courtroom. But they were there for moral support, and God, how she appreciated them.

In the hallway, the world seemed to stop.

Nicole leaned against the wood-paneled wall.

Tripp approached slowly. Their breath collided.

"We're at war," he murmured.

She didn't disagree.

"You gave a potent opening," he said, voice low.

"I didn't come here to impress you," she replied, voice flat.

He tilted his head. "You saw yourself in her."

She shook her head, knowing she was lying.

"You did," he pressed, and she felt the confession unsheathed in her chest.

"Bianca and Mr. Reddick remind me of us," she said softly. "A rich family and a middle-class one. Parents who disagreed with his decision. A poor innocent child killed before it had a chance to survive," she said.

His eyes widened and his body tensed.

"Nicole, if you tell me you were pregnant, I'll lose my shit right here in this courthouse," he said, his voice tight with anger.

"No, I wasn't pregnant. But the similarities are there."

"No, they're not," he defended.

"Oh? Were your mother and father accepting of me? Then why in the hell are we not still married?"

She'd had enough, and she didn't want to be seen talking to him, so she turned and pushed through the door outside to the existing world. One that didn't have a dead, young woman she couldn't help but compare herself to. One where she was a single woman who didn't trust men because of the hurt she'd experienced as a young girl.

A hurt that at least hadn't gotten her killed.

The courtroom was humming with quiet tension, the kind that settled beneath your skin like static. Tripp sat at the defense table, reviewing notes, his pen tapping a silent rhythm against the legal pad in front of him. Judge Price had called for a short break before their next witness took the stand. Nicole was across the aisle, conferring with her second chair, a crease between her brows as she gestured toward the autopsy report.

God, she was laser-focused. And brilliant. He hated how much he still admired that about her. Seeing her at her best gutted him. Not because she was dazzling, he'd always known that, but because they belonged together. He'd always recognized she was smarter than him, but to see her now made him remember all the good times they had together.

And soon, he was going to learn who had ripped them apart.

The courtroom door creaked open, and Tripp glanced up, more out of habit than curiosity, and then he saw her.

His mother.

Suzanne Masterson entered with her signature posture: spine straight, chin slightly lifted like she was inspecting the gallery for dust. She was dressed in a tailored ivory suit and pearl earrings, her silver-gray hair swept into a neat twist. Not a strand out of place.

Her gaze swept over the room, found him, and she smiled as if she were walking into a charity gala, not a murder trial.

Shit.

He hadn't invited her. He hadn't even told her which courtroom he'd be in. And yet, here she was, taking a seat in the second row with that same regal grace she'd weaponized his entire childhood.

Tripp sighed and looked down at his notes again, but his grip on the pen tightened.

Perfect—that makes it sharper.

The trial resumed, and Nicole called her next witness, Bianca's best friend, a young woman with wary eyes and a voice that trembled as she swore the oath.

Nicole stood. Calm. Controlled. Every movement deliberate.

"Tell us about Bianca's last days. Did she fear for her life?"

"Yes," the young woman whispered. "Bianca was afraid of Derrick's family. They told him she wasn't the kind of woman he should be with."

"Was the pregnancy planned?"

"Oh, no. But Bianca used to say there were no accidents. She believed what happened was meant to be. She said she wasn't going to let a baby stop her from going to law school."

"Did Mr. Reddick support the pregnancy?" Nicole asked, her tone sharp enough to cut glass.

The witness shook her head. "He pressured her to get an abortion."

Nicole tilted her head. "But abortion is illegal in Texas, isn't it?"

"He said it didn't matter. He offered to pay for her to fly to Colorado. He even bought the ticket. But Bianca refused. After that, she told me she was thinking of ending things. She said she'd need child support, but she couldn't stay with a man who didn't want their baby."

"And did Mr. Reddick know she was ending the relationship?"

The young woman's hands twisted in her lap. "Yes. The night before she died. She called me right after he left. Said he was furious, accused her of cheating. Said it wasn't his baby. He told her he'd demand a DNA test once the child was born."

"How did Bianca sound?"

Her voice cracked. "She was crying. She said she loved him, but she never thought he'd act that way about their child. She told me she felt crushed by Derrick, by his family, by life. She didn't know if she could trust him anymore."

The courtroom was hushed, Nicole's questions landing like hammer blows. Every juror's gaze was locked on the witness. Every word carried weight.

Tripp sat at the defense table, jaw tight, his gaze fixed on Nicole. She wielded the testimony like a scalpel. Precise. Ruthless. And his mother, seated two rows back, was watching, studying Nicole, and analyzing him. He could feel it like heat on the back of his neck.

When the judge nodded his way, Tripp rose. He buttoned his jacket and stepped toward the witness stand. His shoes clicked on the polished floor, loud in the silence.

"You were Bianca's closest friend, correct?"

"Yes."

"You're not friends with Derrick?"

"No. I'm beneath his social class."

Tripp let the answer hang, then clipped his words. "Just answer the questions, please. Did you like Derrick?"

The young woman hesitated, flicking her gaze toward Nicole. Nicole gave the faintest nod, almost imperceptible, but Tripp saw it. A signal.

"No," the witness said.

"Why not?"

"Because I thought Derrick was using my friend. She was smart, beautiful. He wanted her to help him through college, with sex on the side."

"You didn't believe he loved her?"

"No."

"Did Derrick cheat on Bianca?"

"Not that I know of."

"Did Bianca cheat on him?"

"Never. She was crazy in love with him."

Tripp narrowed his eyes. "Did she want his money?"

Nicole was on her feet in an instant. "Objection. Argumentative."

"Sustained," the judge said.

Tripp pivoted, unruffled. "Bianca didn't come from wealth, did she?"

"No."

"How was she paying for college?"

"Loans and scholarships."

"And yet she lived in a house?"

"It was her grandmother's."

Tripp moved a step closer, voice firm. "Isn't it true that Derrick paid the overdue property taxes on that house?"

Nicole shot up again. "Objection. Relevance."

The judge considered, then waved a hand. "Overruled. The witness may answer."

The young woman exhaled sharply. "Yes—"

Tripp cut her off with a raised hand before she could elaborate. "Just yes or no."

"Yes."

He turned, facing the jury, making sure his voice was steady, commanding. "No further questions, Your Honor."

He walked back to the defense table, every step deliberate. From the corner of his eye, he caught his mother leaning forward, her lips pressed tightly, her gaze flicking between him and Nicole. Judgment in her eyes. Judgment, and something else he couldn't quite read.

And Nicole, she didn't even glance at him. She just slid back into her seat, pen poised, expression carved from stone.

The air between them was thick with unfinished history.

When the jury was dismissed for the day and Judge Price gave his usual admonishment—"Ladies and gentlemen, remember: do not speak about the case with anyone, and do not consume any media coverage."

Tripp was already shoving his files into his briefcase, praying he could slip out before…

"Darling."

He closed his eyes for one beat too long. When he opened them, there she was at the edge of the bar. His mother. Standing tall, smiling like she'd just watched him win the Super Bowl.

"Mother," he said evenly, tamping down the groan rising in his throat. "What are you doing here?"

"I wanted to see my brilliant son in action." She leaned in, kissed his cheek, her perfume a heady mixture of roses and memory. "You haven't taken a high-profile trial in ages. How could I resist? And what an exciting one."

Of course. To her, murder trials were cocktail party fodder.

He studied her face, but as always, the armor was flawless. No cracks in the perfectly polished exterior. "You tracked down my schedule."

"Of course, I did," she said smoothly. "I'm your mother."

"Meaning you called Lorraine at the office and bullied her into telling you."

She fluttered her hand, dismissing the accusation like lint on her jacket. "Details, darling. You were magnificent, by the way. Calm. Measured. I'm proud of you."

That word still stung. Proud. Always conditional. Contingent on obedience.

They walked into the hallway, where the hum of fluorescent lights softened against the blue wash of dusk outside the windows.

"I don't have time to chat," he said, adjusting his pace, hoping she'd fall away.

"I won't keep you long," she promised, falling in step anyway. "But I do have thoughts."

"Of course, you do."

"This girl," she began, and he stiffened at her tone. That same cloying disdain she'd once used for Nicole. "This Bianca Laurent, she reminds me far too much of her."

Tripp stopped cold. "Nicole?"

"She practically cloned her. Pretty. From the wrong side of town. Ambitious in all the wrong ways."

His jaw clenched. "Bianca was shot in the chest, Mom. She and her unborn baby were murdered."

Her eyes narrowed, disdain cutting sharper than grief. "Don't be dramatic. I'm saying she had an agenda. Girls like that always do. Just like Nicole. Always angling for more than they deserve."

The words hit like a fist. *More than they deserve.*

"More than they deserve?" His voice was raw, low. "What exactly do you think Nicole 'deserved,' Mother?"

"Oh, come now, Dustin. You were about to start college. You had your future mapped out. And she—you were both just children. She tried to trap you with that ridiculous wedding. Do you really think she would've waited for marriage unless she had a bigger plan in place?"

The air thickened. Tripp turned to her slowly, heat building in his throat. "You knew."

Her smile faltered, just slightly.

His voice dropped, dangerous. "You knew about the wedding?"

A beat of silence. Too long.

Then her chin tilted, recovering, her expression smoothing into practiced denial. "Don't be ridiculous. Paige told me after it happened."

"No," Tripp said, his chest tight, the realization dawning like a storm. "You said Nicole tried to 'trap' me. That's not how Paige described it. That's *your* word. You knew before. You knew exactly what we were doing that night."

Her lips pressed into a thin, brittle line.

For once, she had no ready dismissal.

She hesitated, eyes flicking away for just a second, then back. "Fine. Yes. I suspected. Paige's mother figured it out, and we pressured your friend until she told us. You were being foolish, Dustin. Someone had to stop you before you threw away everything."

The air went still. Cold. Lifeless.

"You meddled," he said. "You didn't just interfere. You manipulated everything. My father put me on a plane. You had my bags packed. And Nicole, she never got my calls, Mom."

His voice broke.

His mother's eyes softened for just a moment, like a chink in armor. "We were trying to protect you."

"From what?" he demanded. "From loving someone? From choosing a life that didn't fit your mold?"

"She wasn't right for you. She was never going to fit. You had everything ahead of you, and she would have dragged you down."

"You never gave her a chance," he said. "You made that decision for me. For us."

And then it hit him.

The email. The annulment papers. The silence.

He stared at her, horrified. "It was you. You sent that email from my account. You deleted the voicemails. You— God—did you forge her signature on the annulment?"

Her mouth twitched.

"I never meant for you to hate her," she whispered.

"But I did," he said, voice like gravel. "For twenty years."

He turned and walked away, the courtroom doors closing behind him like the end of a sentence. His mother called after him, "Dustin!"

But he didn't turn around.

The truth wasn't clean. It wasn't noble. It was wrapped in manipulation and dressed in pearls.

And now, the woman sitting across the aisle from him in court, the one he'd loved with his whole stupid heart, had suffered just as much as he had because of the same person.

His mother.

CHAPTER 9

$\mathcal{N}$icole had seen her the moment she walked into the courtroom.

The witch herself. Mrs. Masterson.

She sat in the gallery like a queen in exile, pearls gleaming at her throat, hair lacquered into submission. Regal, controlled, watching every move Nicole made. And though she hadn't spoken, Nicole had felt the silent verdict in her eyes: unworthy. Always unworthy.

At the end of the day, she saw the witch talking to Tripp. Good. She didn't want to speak to her ever again, if she could help herself. She walked down the hall to her office, dropped off some paperwork, checked phone messages, then headed out the door to the parking lot. Time to get out of here.

She lugged her briefcase, files, and marched toward the parking lot.

Then she froze.

Mrs. Masterson was there. Waiting. Perfectly poised beside Nicole's car as if she had every right to be standing guard.

Nicole's stomach tightened. *Ambush.*

She squared her shoulders and kept her tone clipped. "Excuse me. You're standing by my car."

The older woman didn't budge. "Nicole, we need to talk."

The sound of her name in that tone was a lash across the skin. Nicole crossed her arms. "About what? I have nothing to say to you. You got what you wanted twenty years ago. You broke Tripp and me apart."

Mrs. Masterson sighed, the picture of weary patience. "What's in the past should remain there. Digging it up serves no one."

Nicole barked a short laugh. "That's convenient. Sweep the wreckage under the rug and pretend it never happened? Tell me, are you afraid Tripp will be angry when he finds out you interfered? Or is this really about you being terrified we might find our way back to each other?" She leaned closer, eyes narrowed. "Still not good enough for your precious son?"

Mrs. Masterson's smile didn't falter, but her eyes sharpened. "You mistake me. My only concern has ever been Tripp's happiness. And frankly, you were never suited to the life he deserves. You were... how shall I put it? A distraction. Pretty enough. Ambitious. But not the kind of woman who could build a future with him."

The words sliced through Nicole, hot and merciless.

She forced herself to stand straighter, though her fists itched to clench. "And who decides what kind of woman is worthy? You?"

Mrs. Masterson's lips curved faintly, an almost pitying smile. "He's dating someone now. A young woman from a very fine family. Educated. Polished. She understands him. She belongs in his world."

The splinter lodged deeper. Tripp hadn't mentioned anyone, but the fact that his mother was flaunting it felt like a deliberate blow.

Nicole laughed, sharp and brittle. "You are afraid. Well, let me put your fears to rest. I don't want Tripp or his baggage, which includes you. I have a good life, one I built without your approval or your money." Her voice cracked with steel. "Sad, isn't it? Once, I loved your son more than life itself. But that's long gone. Now, we're just two lawyers battling in court. Nothing more. And your son sure doesn't look happy to me."

For the briefest moment, Mrs. Masterson's smile faltered, her mask slipping before sliding neatly back into place. "Good. Because Tripp deserves peace. Stability. Not someone who brings… drama in her wake."

Nicole bristled. "You mean not someone who ever dared love him on her own terms."

The pearls at Mrs. Masterson's throat glinted as she tilted her head. "I mean not someone who would ruin him."

The words landed with brutal finality.

Nicole stepped in, closing the space between them until only inches remained. "You don't intimidate me anymore.

Not like you did back then. And just so we're clear, in this courtroom, your son doesn't get a crown. And when this trial is over, he will lose to me. Badly."

For the first time, Mrs. Masterson's expression hardened, the pearls of her composure straining. Then she stepped back, smoothing her skirt with slow precision. "So be it. Just remember, Nicole, when this is over, win or lose, you'll still be on the outside. You always will be. I'll never accept you and your trashy family. Who, by the way, played their role in your separation."

The words ripped through her like a blade, sharp and merciless. She'd feared it, dreaded it, but hearing it from this woman's mouth was agony, each syllable a fresh stab, carving her open until she could barely breathe.

Nicole shoved past her, hand on the driver's door. She slid into the seat, started the car, and gripped the wheel until her knuckles whitened.

Mrs. Masterson lingered, that same faint, pitying smile flickering once more before she turned and glided away.

How did this woman still do it? How, after all these years, could she crawl under Nicole's skin and leave her shaking? Why couldn't she just dismiss her for what she was, a bitter, controlling society matron desperate to control her son's life?

Nicole let her forehead rest against the wheel. A tear slid down her cheek before she could stop it.

And then, inevitably, came the image of Tripp. His steady eyes, the way he carried himself in the courtroom, the quiet strength she used to lean on.

She had sworn she was done with him. Those twenty years of pain had taught her better. But the truth pressed hard against her heart: she wasn't as free as she wanted to believe.

She was still fighting battles that had started decades ago, against him, against his mother, against herself.

And sitting there, alone in her car with her hands trembling on the wheel, Nicole wondered if she would ever stop.

What was she doing?

CHAPTER 10

By the time she turned onto her parents' street, the fury still sat hot under her skin, coiled tightly in her chest. The little Craftsman house looked precisely the same as it had when she was seventeen, the peeling paint, the sagging porch step, the wild rosebush threatening to swallow the windows. How could the house look unchanged when her whole world had tilted?

Even though she was here for her parents, she was beginning to doubt that she should have returned. Staying in Austin would have been the better choice, and yet, her parents needed her.

And yet, she'd just had confirmation that they had helped split up her and Tripp.

Inside, the air smelled of roast chicken and lemon cleaner, a combination that was both ordinary and maddening. Her mother sat at the kitchen table with her crossword puzzle, glasses perched on her nose. Her father sat behind his newspaper, half-listening to the evening news droning from the television in the living room.

"You're home early," her mother said without looking up.

Nicole set her briefcase down harder than she meant to, the thud making both parents glance her way. "Trial let out. Jury's gone home for the day."

Her father folded his newspaper. "How's it going?"

She barked out a laugh, bitter and sharp. "Besides the ghost of high school showing up in the front row?"

They both frowned. But it was more than that; it was the cruel reflection of her own past, a case so eerily like her life that it clawed at her like a ghost she could never outrun.

"Mrs. Masterson," Nicole snapped. "She was there. Watching me. Smiling like she still owns me. Like she still owns everything in this town, including her son."

Her mother made a faint, dismissive sound. "She always did think she was better than everyone else."

The rage was just beneath the surface. It was all she could do to keep it contained.

"And then when I walked out to the parking lot, she was waiting for me. Waiting to warn me to stay away from her son. That I'm still not worthy enough for him. How he's dating someone else. But the worst thing she told me was how my own parents played a part in ending our marriage."

Her mother gasped.

Nicole's chest burned. "It's not just her. This case, it's

like looking into a mirror. A girl who loves the wrong boy. A family who wants her gone. I'm standing in court reliving my own nightmare, only now the names are Bianca and Derrick instead of Nicole and Tripp."

Her father shifted in his chair. "Nicole—"

She whirled on him. "Don't. Don't you dare. I know exactly what you thought back then. That I was too young, too naïve, that Tripp Masterson would never actually marry me. But we did, and then you interfered."

The words cracked through the kitchen like a whip.

Silence. The kind that made the clock on the wall tick louder, the refrigerator hum too sharply.

Her mother took off her glasses and folded them with careful precision, as if buying time. "We only wanted what was best for you."

Nicole's pulse stumbled. "What does that mean?"

Her father cleared his throat, eyes dropping to the table. "Sometimes parents have to make choices their children don't understand."

Her heart lurched, cold flooding her veins. "Choices?" Her voice rose, raw. "Are you telling me that she's right? That my own parents had something to do with the annulment?"

Her mother's hand clenched, the pencil in her grip snapping clean in two.

The sound was small, but it detonated inside Nicole.

Her father looked at the broken pencil, then at her. His expression sagged with guilt. "We thought we were protecting you."

Nicole reeled back, a sob catching in her throat. "Protecting me? From what? From love? From the only boy I ever—" She cut herself off, but the words hung between them, alive and sharp.

Her mother's chair screeched as she pushed it back. "Do not raise your voice to me, Nicole."

It was a defense move. She was trying to make her feel like a child again, but it wasn't going to work.

Nicole's laugh was jagged, half-hysterical. "Don't raise my voice? You admit you destroyed my life, and you want me to keep quiet? You didn't just stand by while Tripp's mother tore us apart, you helped her, didn't you? You stood with her."

Her mother flinched, just barely, but it was enough.

Her father stood abruptly and paced to the sink. He gripped the counter, his shoulders slumped.

"We thought it was the right thing," he said, his voice hoarse.

Nicole's vision blurred with tears. "The right thing? You let me believe for twenty years that I wasn't good enough. That he didn't want me. You let me carry that shame while you sat here eating roast chicken and working crossword puzzles."

"Nicole—" Her mother's voice cracked, sharp with control.

"No!" Nicole's scream shook the air, raw and furious. "Don't you dare try to spin this. Don't you dare tell me you did it for my own good. You lied. You interfered. You—"

The people she trusted above all others had been

tangled in this debacle, betraying her in the worst way. Her throat closed around the words. Rage. Grief. Betrayal. It all choked her until she could barely breathe.

She grabbed her briefcase, her fingers trembling. "I can't look at either of you right now."

Her father turned, anguish on his face. "Please, just let us explain—"

"No!" She backed toward the door, her chest heaving. "You've had twenty years to explain. And you said nothing. Nothing!"

Her mother reached out a hand, but Nicole yanked the door open, hot air rushing in.

"If you really thought you were protecting me," she choked out, "then you never knew me at all. I loved Tripp, and he loved me until you ripped us apart."

The door slammed behind her, rattling the windows.

Outside, the evening air was heavy and hot, cicadas screaming in the trees. Nicole strode to her car, tears spilling unchecked, her whole body trembling.

For years, she had believed Tripp had left her because he didn't love her enough and it was her fault.

Now she knew better.

And the truth was so much worse. There was only one person she could talk to about this, but she didn't know how to reach him, except through his law office.

But Paige…Paige would know.

CHAPTER 11

The city blurred past his windshield, neon streaks bending in the glass as if the whole world had slanted. Tripp drove too fast, his jaw aching from how tightly he clenched it. He should have gone straight to his office, buried himself in case files, drowned in work until the heat of his mother's revelations cooled. But the storm inside him wouldn't quiet.

His mother's words clung like smoke.

She tried to trap you. That ridiculous wedding. You had your future mapped out.

She had known. All along, she had known.

His hands tightened on the steering wheel until his knuckles throbbed. For twenty years, he had carried the belief that Nicole had walked away. That she had chosen ambition over him. That she hadn't loved him enough. He'd used that betrayal like armor, every late night, every long case, every wall he built around his heart.

He'd even married a nice girl, trying to forget Nicole. Hoping that Anna would somehow wipe his mind clear of the girl he'd loved. But all he'd done was hurt her in the end.

And today, in the span of a few careless sentences, his mother had ripped it all apart.

As the sun dipped below the horizon, he knew there was no more running from the truth. He had to go home and confront his mother.

The streetlights flickered over him as he drove, throwing shadows across the dashboard. His chest heaved, fury pressing against his ribs like it wanted out. He saw flashes of Nicole in his mind, her laugh, bright and reckless, the way she used to kiss him under the bleachers like they were the only two people in the world.

And the way she'd looked at him in court today, sharp, unflinching, refusing to back down.

She didn't leave me, he thought savagely. *She was* taken *from me.*

The thought burned through him, scorching away twenty years of certainty.

He didn't realize where he was driving until he pulled into the long circular drive of the family estate. The house loomed in the darkness, sprawling and immaculate, every window glowing with warm light. To the world, it was a picture of elegance. To Tripp, it had always been a gilded cage.

A cage he was living in, but starting tomorrow, he'd hire a real estate agent to find him a house. A place of his own. It was time to move out and move on. He'd only moved in to help his mother with the grief of his father, but the woman wasn't grieving; she was conniving.

The boy who had once adored his mother could never have fathomed the cruelty she was capable of, the depths of evil she would embrace. You don't imagine that of the people meant to love you, the ones you trust to want your happiness. And realizing it now felt like having the very ground ripped out from under him, leaving nothing but betrayal where love had once been.

He killed the engine, sat in silence, breath harsh in his throat. He could have turned around. Should have. But fury propelled him forward. He slammed the car door and strode up the stone steps, his shoes echoing in the humid night.

The front door opened before he could open it. Of course, she'd heard the car. His mother stood framed in the light, a glass of wine in hand, pearls catching the glow.

"You're home," she said as though she'd summoned him.

"Right now, I live here, but not for long," he snapped, brushing past her into the foyer.

She shut the door with quiet grace, the click of the latch loud in the cavernous entryway. "You're upset."

He spun on her, fury sparking. "Upset? You let me live for twenty years believing Nicole left me. You *knew* what we were planning, and you ended it."

Her expression flickered, the faintest tremor, before the mask slid back into place. "I was protecting you."

"Protecting me?" His voice cracked. "From what? From being happy? From the only woman I've ever loved?"

Her tone sharpened. "From throwing away your future. You were a boy, Dustin, blinded by hormones and puppy love. That girl would have ruined your life."

His fists clenched. "She was my life."

His mother's eyes narrowed. "No. The Masterson name is your life. The firm. The legacy. That girl didn't belong in our world, and you know it. She's made good, but she still is beneath you."

Even now, Nicole wasn't enough for her. In his mother's world, the only woman fit to be his wife was one she handpicked, some polished puppet she could control. Like that blonde she'd dragged to dinner the other night, dull as dishwater and twice as forgettable. He couldn't even recall her name, and the fact his mother thought she was suitable made his blood boil.

Better single forever than shackled to one of her puppets.

Tripp laughed, jagged and bitter. "You're wrong. She belonged more than you ever did. She was kind. She was real. Everything you can't even pretend to be."

Her nostrils flared, the stem of her wineglass trembling in her hand. "Mind your tone. I am your mother."

He stepped closer, fury radiating off him. "No. For once, you're going to hear me. You lied. You let me believe Nicole chose to walk away. You made me hate her for something she didn't do. Do you know what that did to me?"

Her lips thinned. "It made you strong. Cold. Exactly what this world requires."

Oh my God, she wanted him to be shattered. Her own words. It was like someone ripped the blinders from his eyes, and for the first time, he saw her clearly. Not as his mother, but as the cold-hearted bitch she truly was, a woman who cared only for wealth and power.

His chest heaved. "No. It made me empty."

The silence that followed was suffocating. The chandelier above threw fractured light across the marble floor, gilding the distance between them. His mother lifted her chin, her mask of composure cracking just slightly at the edges.

"You'll thank me one day," she said softly, her voice honey over steel.

Tripp stared at her, the woman who had orchestrated his life like a chessboard, moving pieces in secret while he bled for her victories. His voice dropped to a dangerous whisper. "Don't hold your breath."

He turned, yanked the front door open, and strode out into the night. The door slammed behind him, the sound echoing like finality.

He sat in his car in the driveway, the leather seat hot beneath him, his breath ragged. The house loomed in the rearview mirror, glowing with all the false warmth. He couldn't stay here tonight.

For twenty years, he had lived inside a lie. His mother had stolen his past, rewritten it, twisted it into something that had fueled his ambition but hollowed him out inside.

God, how he wanted to speak to Nicole. To find her, to sit across from her, and finally untangle how it had all gone so wrong. But they couldn't—not in public. Not until the trial was over, or risk handing the judge a reason for a mistrial. So he bit back the urge, even as the past clawed at him, fierce and relentless, begging to be dragged into the light.

The past was a grave he'd thought long buried. Tonight, it cracked open, and everything inside clawed its way out. All the ugliness, but not the details. Sooner or later, he had to have the details of how they had carried out this devious plot that destroyed their happiness.

He sat there for a long time, the cicadas screaming in the humid night air, headlights washing over his car as neighbors came and went.

Finally, he drew in a shuddering breath. He couldn't sit here drowning in the wreckage. He needed answers. Paige had come back and was doing her best to learn what she could about that night. Tonight, he needed to talk to her.

Before he could second-guess himself, he shoved the key into the ignition. The engine roared to life, headlights slicing through the darkness. He pulled away from the house, gravel spitting under his tires.

This time, he wasn't driving to outrun the past.

This time, he was driving straight into it, a storm of truth and betrayal that churned inside him like a hurricane, every gust threatening to tear him apart. At its center stood his mother, cold and immovable, feeding the winds with her lies. And circling just as fiercely was Nicole, the only woman he'd ever loved, the one he'd lost, the one he might never reclaim.

He gripped the wheel tighter, bracing for impact, knowing there was no way out, only straight through the heart.

The ocean whispered outside Paige's rented beach house, steady and relentless, like it had all the answers Nicole couldn't find. She sat curled on the sagging couch, bare toes buried in the throw blanket, a mug of tea cooling in her hands.

Outside, it was hot, but Nicole was shaking inside and out from what she'd learned tonight.

Inside, her nerves quaked like a nine-point earthquake, splintering her. She'd prepared herself to face the truth about Mrs. Masterson, that much she had always suspected. But her own parents? That betrayal struck like a collapse she hadn't seen coming, crushing her in ways she didn't know she could survive.

If she couldn't trust them, who was left?

"I don't know what to think anymore," she said, her voice raw. "Everything I thought I knew about what happened with Tripp…about why we ended…it's unraveling."

Paige sat on the cushion next to her. She didn't press, didn't pity, just waited.

Nicole's throat ached as she forced the words out. "Mrs. Masterson was waiting for me in the parking lot after court today."

Paige's eyes snapped up, sharp with concern.

Nicole gave a laugh, jagged and brittle. "The woman warned me away from her son. Said he had a girlfriend who was exactly the kind of woman he needed." The sound dissolved into silence, bitter as ash.

"That's not true," Paige said quickly, almost too quickly, like she needed to defend Tripp. "Or at least…he hasn't told me about one."

Nicole lifted her teacup with trembling hands, the china rattling against its saucer. She took a sip, though the liquid scalded going down. "Well, whether it's true or not, she wanted me to hear it. To cut me down. To remind me I'm not good enough. And then—" her voice cracked, splintering— "then she dropped a bomb on me."

Paige's posture stiffened, wary. "What?"

Nicole gripped the cup so tightly, she was afraid she'd shatter it. "She told me my parents helped her break up me and Tripp."

Paige blinked, stunned. Her lips parted, then closed, then opened again. Finally, she shook her head. "Dear God. That woman is a witch."

And that was all it took, the final blow. Nicole's breath hitched, and a sob broke free. Tears slipped hot and fast down her cheeks, falling into her tea. "I went home after court and confronted Mom and Dad. I told them about running into Mrs. Masterson, about how this case feels like a mirror of everything I lost with Tripp. And I told them I *knew*." Her voice cracked again, her words breaking into shards.

Paige leaned across the couch, her hand covering Nicole's in a firm, grounding hold.

Nicole shook her head, fighting for air. "They didn't deny it, Paige. Not outright. They as much as admitted it. That they had something to do with it. The breakup." Her chest heaved. "They wouldn't give me details, but it was enough. Enough to know they're guilty. That they—" She swallowed, the word tasting like blood. "That they lied to me."

Paige's fingers tightened around hers. "Oh, Nicole…"

"All these years," Nicole sobbed, pressing her palms to her eyes. "I thought it was just Tripp. That he'd stopped loving me. That he'd walked away. And now I find out my *own parents*, the two people I believed most, helped destroy us."

Paige pulled her closer, wrapping an arm around Nicole's shoulders, pulling her into the steady warmth of a friend's embrace. Nicole sagged against her, the fight draining out of her.

Why did it feel like this had been the battle of her life?

Paige's voice was gentle but sure. "You were their

shining star, and Tripp was a threat to them, Nicole. None of that was your fault. Not then. Not now."

Nicole let out a shaky laugh through her tears, muffled against Paige's shoulder. "Then why does it feel like everything was my fault?"

"Because they wanted what was best for you, and they believed that you and Tripp were too young to know what you wanted," Paige said fiercely, brushing a tear from Nicole's cheek. "But you were loved. You *are* loved. And you've carried the weight of this for far too long."

Nicole clung to her, sobs breaking free again, her body trembling with twenty years of buried pain.

For the first time in years, she didn't feel like she was drowning alone.

Paige's eyes darkened. "Oh, Nic."

Nicole set the mug down before her hands betrayed the tremor in them. "I've spent twenty years believing Tripp left me, that he didn't love me enough. That I wasn't good enough. And now—" Her voice cracked. "Now I don't know what to believe."

The screen door creaked. Nicole turned, expecting the salty wind. Instead—

Tripp.

He stood in the doorway, framed by the ocean in the distance, shoulders tense, eyes locked on her. For a heartbeat, the world held still, the only sound the tide rushing against the shore. The waves crashing onto the beach, like her life was unraveling around her.

"Did you call him?"

"No," Paige said. "I told him where I'm staying, but I didn't know he was coming over tonight."

"I need answers," he said. "And Paige was the only person I thought could give them to me. But I'm so happy you're here."

Paige looked between them. Then, with a slight nod, she rose. "I'll give you two some privacy." She slipped out the back door, leaving silence in her wake.

Nicole's pulse thundered. "What are you doing here?"

"I could ask you the same," he said, his voice rough. He stepped inside, closing the door behind him. "But I think we both came for the same reason."

She swallowed. "Answers?"

"I came here after I left my mother's," he said. "I didn't know you would be here."

Nicole folded her arms. "So what? This is fate? Us ending up in the same place on the same night?"

"Not fate." His eyes were fierce. "Truth. Finally."

The word cracked open something inside her. She sank back on the couch, gesturing stiffly. "Fine. Sit. Let's get it out."

He sat across from her, leaning forward, forearms braced on his knees. For a long moment, neither spoke, twenty years of silence pressing down like a weight.

Finally, Nicole broke. "I thought you left me." Her voice wavered. "I thought you didn't want me anymore."

His jaw clenched. "And I thought you walked away. Chose college. Chose anything but me."

She drew in a shaky breath. "I never walked away. I was

crushed that summer. All our plans, and yet you weren't speaking to me. Suddenly, you wanted to party in college. You wanted anyone but me."

Tripp turned to face her, his eyes darkened, and his mouth turned down.

"No, I thought you didn't want me," he said, his voice cracking. "I was in Europe. I couldn't reach you by phone. Not even email."

"As I said before, I never got your calls," Nicole said, her throat raw, her voice shaking with old hurt. "All I got was that email, the one that said you wanted to party your way through college, that you wanted to date other women. Even today, your mother cornered me and told me you were seeing someone *appropriate*."

Tripp froze, disbelief flashing across his face. "What?" His voice was sharp, incredulous, as though the word itself was dragged from his gut.

She told him. Every last detail. The ambush in the parking lot, the way Mrs. Masterson had looked her in the eye and warned her away, and worst of all, the revelation about her parents. Nicole's chest tightened with every word, but she pushed them out anyway, because he deserved to hear it, even if it shattered them both.

There would be no more secrets.

By the time she finished, Tripp's face was scarlet with fury. His jaw clenched so hard, a muscle ticked in his cheek, and his fists balled at his sides. He looked like he could put his fist through a wall.

"Damn," he ground out, dragging both hands down his

face. He paced once, then stopped in front of her, his voice breaking. "Nicole, I never wrote that email. Not one damn word of it. I was in Europe, trying to call you every chance I got. Then my phone disappeared. I lost every number, and when I came back—" His voice cracked, and he swallowed hard. "When I came back, you were gone. And I thought..." He shook his head, anguish twisting his features. "I thought you didn't want me anymore."

Her heart pounded, the ground tilting beneath her.

"I'm sorry," he whispered, his voice thick. He reached for her hand, then stopped himself, his fingers curling into a fist instead. "God, Nicole, I am so damn sorry. For all of it. For not finding a way to break through. For letting them come between us. I would have burned the world down to keep you if I'd known."

Nicole's breath caught, the weight of his confession pressing down on her chest until she thought she might shatter under it. For a heartbeat, she wanted to believe him, God, every cell in her body ached to believe him. His voice, his eyes, the raw truth etched in his face...it all rang with sincerity.

But then the memories crashed back. The sleepless nights. The hollow ache of waiting for calls that never came. The email that had sliced her open. The twenty years of wondering why she wasn't enough.

Her hands trembled as she clasped them tighter. "Do you have any idea what it did to me?" she whispered, her voice breaking. "I thought you'd chosen every party, every girl, over me. I thought I was disposable. And you weren't there to tell me otherwise."

A sob clawed its way up her throat, and she pressed a fist against her mouth, trying to hold it back. "You say you didn't write that email, but I lived with it. I *believed* it. For two decades, I believed you didn't want me, Tripp."

Her eyes burned as she met his, hot tears spilling freely now. "So you'll have to forgive me if it's not so easy to just…believe. Because if I let myself believe you now, it means I wasted twenty years hating you when I should have hated *them*."

Her voice broke on the last word, her shoulders shaking under the weight of all she'd carried alone.

"I never stopped loving you." His voice cracked, raw. He scrubbed a hand down his face. "My mother admitted it all tonight. She knew we had eloped. She wanted it ended. That's why they were waiting for me to come home. My bags were packed and the plane was waiting for us to arrive at the airport."

Nicole's breath hitched. "My parents too. They didn't say how, but they said they were protecting me."

He let out a jagged laugh. "That's the same word my mother used."

They stared at each other, anger and grief thick between them. Finally, Nicole whispered, "We were kids. We trusted them. And they lied."

His gaze softened, pained. "They stole twenty years from us. Twenty years that I longed for you."

She gasped. "I never married. No one ever compared to you."

He sighed. "I married, hoping she would erase you from my mind, but it didn't work. She quickly realized she wasn't the one I longed for."

Nicole pressed her fingers to her temples. "God, Tripp, I keep replaying that night in my head. The two of us were so excited when we left the party and went to that chapel. I was shaking so hard, I could barely say the vows. We promised each other forever, and then it was nothing."

His lips curved with something like grief and memory. "That old Mustang. I'd spent all day cleaning it out, making it perfect for you. You looked like—" He broke off, his voice unsteady. "You looked like the rest of my life."

Her throat closed. She remembered the way his hand had gripped hers, both of them giddy and terrified. How they'd driven toward the chapel, headlights cutting through the dark, whispering plans like fairy tales. And how suddenly it had all come crashing to an end.

"I waited all day for you," she whispered. "We were going to tell our parents. When you didn't show, I thought,

I thought you'd changed your mind. And then I received your email, and it crushed me."

"They gave me no choice. Get in the limo; we're leaving. I had no idea where we were going. I had no idea we were going to fly to Europe. I had no idea we would be gone all summer." His eyes burned. "But it wasn't us, Nic. It was them. They made sure we never had the chance to fulfill the promises we made to each other."

Her hands trembled in her lap. "I wasted half my life hating you."

"And I wasted mine believing you didn't want me."

The words landed like stones, heavy with years of regret.

Slowly, Tripp reached across the space and covered her hand with his. His touch was tentative but searing, like an anchor and a spark all at once.

"Let's start here," he said. "With me. With you. With us. Talking. Finally talking."

Nicole's eyes burned, but she didn't pull away. For the first time in two decades, the walls cracked.

They pieced together fragments. Her parents' evasions. His mother's slips. The way neither story made sense unless both families had been involved. They filled in the gaps with memory, with pain, and with the suspicion that there was still more truth buried.

Tripp's jaw hardened. "We can't keep guessing. We need to know exactly what happened that night."

Nicole frowned. "And how do you suggest we do that?"

His eyes met hers, unflinching. "We bring them together. All of them. Your parents. My mother. We make them tell us what they did."

Her stomach dropped. "You really think they'll admit it?"

"They've already admitted enough," he said flatly. "But I'm done living in the dark. We deserve the truth."

The conviction in his voice stole her breath. He wasn't the boy she remembered, impulsive, reckless, full of big dreams. He was a man now. Harder. Colder in some ways. But that fire she'd loved was still there.

Nicole pulled her hand back, pressing it against her chest like she needed to hold her heart in place. "Tripp… this trial. Everything I've worked for is hanging in the balance. If we stir this up now, it'll consume me."

His eyes searched hers. "I want to see you again. Away from all this. Away from court."

Her pulse skipped, aching to say yes. But she shook her head. "Not until after the trial. Believe me, I want to know the truth."

She gazed at him, her eyes brimming with tears. "Maybe we've missed our chance or…"

"No," he said. "Even now, I feel such a strong connection to you. Even now, I know we need time to figure things out."

She reached out and grabbed his hand. "I'd like that. I want the chance to know if what we felt twenty years ago is still possible. This time, we're adults. This time, no one can stop us."

"This time, it will be for us," he said. "God, I want to kiss you."

She shook her head. "No. Because I fear once you kiss me, I won't be able to stop what will happen between us."

A grin spread across his face.

"After the trial is over, I promise you, we'll get our parents together and learn the truth," she said.

"And then we'll see if what we had is still there."

"Yes," she said softly.

His jaw flexed, but after a long pause, he nodded once. "After the trial, then."

The ocean roared outside, relentless and steady, as if to remind her that time always moved forward.

For the first time in twenty years, they were on the same side of the truth.

And that terrified her more than any verdict ever could.

She stood. "I should go."

"Can I walk you to your car?"

"Yes," she said. "Tell Paige, thank you."

A smile crossed his face. "We're naming our first child after her."

A giggle escaped from Nicole, and then he walked her outside. The urge to kiss him was so strong, but she resisted.

"See you in court," she said.

"And I know you won't go easy on me."

"Absolutely not."

CHAPTER 13

The waves hit the shore in long, steady breaths, the sound carrying through the open windows of Paige's rented beach house. The curtains lifted and fell with the night breeze, stirring the smell of salt and the faint trace of coffee that lingered in the air.

Tripp sat at the small kitchen table, hands wrapped around a mug he hadn't touched. He stared down at the swirling reflection of the overhead light in the dark liquid, wishing it were strong whiskey instead.

Paige leaned against the counter, arms folded, watching him with that calm steadiness that had always made it impossible for her to lie to him. They'd been friends during high school. Never dated. Never romantically involved, just friends.

"You two finally talked," she said. It wasn't a question.

Tripp exhaled slowly, dragging a hand across his jaw. "Yeah."

"And?"

"And it changes everything." His voice was rough, words scraping their way out. "All these years, I thought she walked away. I thought she didn't want me. But she didn't walk, Paige. She was pushed. Just like me."

Paige's eyes softened, but her voice was firm. "That's what I always thought. The way you both unraveled…it never sat right with me." She tilted her head. "So now what?"

Tripp blinked at her. "Now what?"

"You're both standing here, face to face with the truth for the first time in twenty years," Paige said, pushing away from the counter. "You've still got feelings. You'd be a fool to deny it. So I'm asking: what happens if you two find your way back to each other?"

The question landed like a stone in his chest. Tripp shifted back in the chair, his jaw tightening. "That's not exactly on the table right now. We're in the middle of a trial."

Paige pulled out the chair opposite him and sat, propping her chin on her hand. "Stop dodging, Tripp. I know you. I watched you two fall in love, remember? I was there when you couldn't keep your hands off each other, when you whispered about the future like you owned it. You're not indifferent. Neither is she."

A muscle worked in his cheek. He didn't deny it. Couldn't.

Paige leaned forward. "So I'll ask again. What happens if you get back together? Because your mother sure as hell isn't going to welcome her with open arms. And I get the feeling her family wasn't exactly accepting of you either."

Tripp's stomach knotted. He could hear his mother's voice even now, sharp as a knife: *Girls like that always want more than they deserve.* He pressed his thumb against the rim of the mug, grounding himself.

"She'll never accept Nicole," he admitted. The words tasted bitter. "She didn't then. She won't now."

"Then the question is simple," Paige said. "Are you willing to watch someone you care about be mistreated by your mother?"

The air seemed to thicken. He swallowed hard. His first instinct was to argue, to say he could handle it, that Nicole was strong enough to handle it too. But Paige's eyes pinned him down, demanding more than the easy answer. And sadly, there wasn't one.

Finally, he shook his head. "No. I'm not willing."

"Good," Paige said softly. "Because if you can't stand up to your mother now, you'll lose Nicole all over again. And this time, she won't come back."

Tripp rubbed the back of his neck, the muscles tight. "You think I don't know that?" He blew out a bitter laugh. "Paige, I've spent half my life hating her. Believing she didn't love me enough to fight. Do you know what that does to a man? To carry that around while you imagine her building a life without you?"

How many nights had he lain awake, tormented by the thought of her in another man's arms? How many times had her name slipped past his lips in the dark, whispered into the wrong woman's hair, a ghost he could never banish? And always—always—he found himself dragged back to the memory of their wedding night, the one perfect moment before it all unraveled. He had clung to it, cursed it, wished himself back inside it with a desperation that hollowed him out.

Paige's gaze softened, but she didn't flinch. "And now you know the truth."

"Yeah. That my mother stole her from me." He looked down at his hands, flexing them open and closed. "It's not just about losing Nicole. It's about losing us. The life we should have had. The years that should have been ours. Graduating from college together. Going to law school, passing the bar, and having a family. By now, we should have had the two-point-five kids we talked about. It may be too late for a family, but damn, I want a little girl with her coloring and a son with her eyes. Damn them!"

The words lodged in his throat, thick and aching. He had never spoken them aloud, never allowed himself to even think them fully. But now that they were out, he couldn't stop.

"I remember that night," he said, voice low. "I remember cleaning out the Mustang, shining it up, making it perfect because I thought I was driving her into forever. She was going to wear that white sundress; she thought it was silly, but she still wore it because she wanted to look like a bride. And then...our wedding night. The next morning, we promised to bring our parents together. But I was a fool. I should never have gotten into that limo."

"Could you have stopped your parents?"

"Probably not," he said. "But I could have refused."

He trailed off, the memory slicing open like a wound.

Paige reached across the table, resting her hand on his. "You weren't a fool. You were betrayed. By the people who should have loved you both the most."

His throat tightened. He looked away, blinking hard against the burn in his eyes.

Paige's voice was softer now. "You've always been strong, Tripp. Always. But this…this is your weakness. And if you want Nicole back, if you even want the chance, you have to decide if you're willing to fight your mother this time. Not argue. Not push back a little. Fight. Because Suzanne Masterson won't give up control without blood."

Her words landed with brutal clarity. He could picture it already, Nicole in his mother's presence, being dismissed with that icy disdain, diminished in every possible way. And Nicole wouldn't take it silently. She'd fight back. Which meant the war would be constant.

Tripp dragged in a deep breath. "Then I'll have to choose Nicole. Every time."

Paige's lips curved into the faintest smile. "Good. Because she deserves nothing less. And so do you."

The silence stretched, broken only by the ocean beyond the windows. For the first time in years, Tripp felt like he'd said something true. Something final.

But it didn't make him feel lighter. It made him feel the weight of what was coming.

Because he knew a war was inevitable, one with his

mother, maybe even with Nicole's parents. Lines had already been drawn, and soon they would all be forced to choose. Either they accepted him and Nicole together, found a way to ask for forgiveness and move on, or they could walk away and stay gone. As for him, there was no choice to make. Right now, all he wanted was Nicole. The rest of them, their judgment, their power, their lies, be damned.

He looked at Paige. "She told me tonight, she won't see me. Not until after the trial."

"Smart," Paige said. "It keeps the lines clean. You're both professionals, and the jury doesn't need to see anything that looks like collusion."

"It's hell," he muttered.

"It's temporary. You've waited twenty years, what's a few more days?" Paige corrected. She leaned back, studying him. "The bigger question is what happens after? If you two manage to dig through this mess and come out standing, what then? Are you ready to let go of the Masterson legacy if it means keeping her?"

Tripp's chest tightened. The firm. The family name. Everything he had been told mattered. He thought of his mother's voice again: *You'll thank me one day.*

Since his father's death, the law firm had been his anchor, his duty, the legacy he was bound to protect. But standing here now, none of it mattered. He would walk away from every polished boardroom, every cent of his inheritance, if it meant a life with Nicole. They could carve out their own future, stripped of expectations and family chains. He didn't care about the firm, the money, or the name he'd been raised to revere. Nicole was all that mattered—she always had been.

And then he thought of Nicole's eyes across the courtroom. Fire. Hurt. Unyielding strength. The woman he wanted to spend forever with.

"Yes," he said finally, the word rough and certain. "If it comes to it, yes."

Paige nodded slowly, as if she'd been waiting to hear him say it. "Then maybe you've finally grown into the man she always saw in you. The man I didn't see, but she did."

Tripp sat back, breath leaving him in a long exhale. Outside, the ocean kept its steady rhythm, the same way it had when they were teenagers sneaking kisses on the beach. Only now, the years between them stretched wide, heavy with what had been stolen.

But for the first time in decades, Tripp felt something other than anger.

He felt resolve. He felt hope. He felt an almost giddy anticipation.

Tomorrow, the trial would continue. Tomorrow, he would have to stand across from Nicole, both of them fighting for opposite sides.

But tonight, he had made his choice. And he wasn't going to let anyone, not his mother, not the Masterson name, not the past, not even her parents, take her away again.

CHAPTER 14

Two days later, Nicole was back at the beach house with her friends. The ocean hummed in the background, a steady rhythm that mixed with the laughter of women and the gentle clink of glasses.

Paige's little beach rental looked lived in now, empty wine bottles lined up like trophies on the counter, throw pillows scattered across the couch from earlier pillow fights, the faint smell of popcorn still lingering. Empty pizza boxes where they'd consumed their favorite meal.

Nicole sat cross-legged on the floor, her back against the sofa, holding her third, or was it her fourth, glass of wine. She'd lost count somewhere around the second bottle, when Crystal had pulled out that ridiculous story about her last blind date, which had them all howling until their sides ached.

"God, I missed this," Paige said, curling up on the armchair with her glass balanced on one knee. The lamplight softened her features, and for the first time, Nicole noticed how relaxed she looked, with no tight shoulders and no careful city polish. Just Paige. Not the prominent city executive who traveled the world.

When she'd first arrived on the island, the signs of wear were written all over her, shadows smudged beneath her eyes, tension bowstring-tight across her shoulders, a stiffness in her every movement. She'd looked like life had taken too much from her. But now…now Nicole caught glimpses of the Paige she remembered. The carefree girl who used to laugh too loudly, danced barefoot in the sand, and lived as though the night would never end.

"You've missed wine?" Crystal teased.

"I've missed *home,*" Paige corrected, sweeping her gaze around the room, then out the window where the dark ocean stretched. "I didn't think I would. Honestly, when I packed to come here, I was planning to count the days until I left again. But now?" She gave a half-shrug, her smile soft. "I don't want to leave."

"Spoken like a true island girl," one of the others said, raising her glass in salute.

Nicole took a sip, hiding her smile. Paige had always been the one who swore she'd never come back, never get stuck in the same small-town cycles. And now here she was, glowing with contentment in a beat-up rental on the beach.

This was the woman who built empires with a pen, who negotiated million-dollar contracts and appeared in glossy business magazines as the face of power and success.

Nicole had always expected her to end up in the corner office of some skyscraper, running a corporation like she was born to it. But here, Paige wasn't the executive powerhouse. Here she was relaxed, radiant even, happier than Nicole had ever seen her. And God help her, Nicole couldn't decide if she admired her for it...or envied her.

Mostly, Nicole was just grateful to call her a friend, and more than anything, she wanted her happiness.

Paige leaned back in her chair, her grin widening. "I mean it. I didn't realize how much I missed this place. The air, the water, the people. Even the gossip. It's... comforting."

"Careful," Amanda teased, "another week and you'll be signing a lease."

"Or buying," Paige said, her tone playful but not entirely joking.

Nicole laughed with the others, but a tiny ache stirred inside her. For years, she'd defined herself by leaving. By proving she could build something outside the island, outside her parents' control, outside Tripp Masterson's shadow. And now Paige, the girl who'd sworn she'd never look back, was talking about coming home.

If she did, it would mean everyone who had once left had somehow found their way back. And maybe, just maybe, that wasn't such a bad thing after all.

Nicole took another long sip. She wasn't about to be the sentimental one tonight. Tonight was about having fun, and she needed this brief respite from the drama in her life and in the courtroom.

The conversation drifted into favorite beaches and worst high school crushes until Paige, a little pink from the wine, blurted, "Well, at least you and Tripp are talking now."

The room went dead silent.

Nicole froze, her glass halfway to her mouth. Paige's eyes widened as if she wanted to swallow the words back, but it was too late. Jennifer leaned forward, brows arched high. "Excuse me?"

Nicole set her glass down carefully, as though the stem might snap in her hand. "It's not what you think."

"Oh, it's *exactly* what I think," Crystal said with a sly grin. "Tripp Masterson. Mister Brooding Defense Attorney. Mister First Love. Mister—"

"Don't," Nicole cut in, sharper than she meant. Her voice cracked through the room, silencing the chuckles. She pressed her fingertips against her glass, grounding herself. "Yes, we talked. Once. That doesn't mean anything. I see him almost every day in court. We're not together again."

Paige bit her lip. "I didn't mean to—"

"It doesn't mean anything," Nicole repeated, though her voice wavered now. "We had to clear the air. That's all. We deserve to know the truth."

Crystal exchanged a look with Amanda, then leaned back with a little smile that said she wasn't fooled.

Nicole forced a laugh, but it came out brittle. "We're on opposite sides of a murder trial, for God's sake. That's not exactly a foundation for..." She trailed off, realizing she was about to say *forever*. She snatched up her wineglass and took a long swallow instead.

The others let it drop, drifting into safer gossip, but Nicole felt Paige's gaze linger on her.

By the time the bottles were empty and the laughter had softened into that warm haze only late-night wine could bring, Paige spoke again. This time, her voice was gentle.

"Nic?"

Nicole leaned back against the sofa cushions, eyelids heavy, glass dangling loosely in her hand. "Mmm?"

"What if it wasn't just talking?"

Nicole's eyes snapped open. Paige's gaze was steady now, the wine flush gone, her tone serious. "What if you and Tripp…found your way back?"

A dozen retorts leaped to Nicole's tongue, the trial, the past, the hurt. But Paige pressed on.

"Could you live with his mother again?"

The words landed like a weight. Nicole sat up straighter, the buzz of wine thinning in an instant. The other girls glanced between them, suddenly alert. How could she ever deal with his mother again?

Paige didn't stop. "I remember what she did to you back then, how she looked at you like you were less. Like you were stealing something that didn't belong to you. Could you really put yourself through that again?"

Nicole's chest tightened. Images flashed, Suzanne Masterson's icy smile, her cutting remarks dressed up as compliments, the way she had once called Nicole *that girl* with a curl of her lip.

Nicole swallowed hard. "I don't know." Her voice was small, raw. "I don't know if I could ever forgive her, if I confirm what she did to me and Tripp."

Crystal leaned in. "And what about your family? After everything that happened, do you think they'd accept him back into your life? Into theirs?"

Nicole pressed her palms to her knees, staring at the rug. Her parents' faces came to mind, the argument in the kitchen only nights ago, the admission that they'd participated. Their duplicity still stung like a fresh wound.

"I don't know if *they* could accept him," she whispered. "I don't know if I could accept them either. I know they did something, but we haven't sat down and talked about what. Right now, I have to focus on this trial and nothing else. And tonight, I need a little fun. A chance to get away from everything."

Silence settled over the group, heavier than the wine, heavier than the night.

Paige reached across and squeezed her hand. "Then maybe that's the real question, Nic. Not whether you and Tripp still love each other. But whether you could survive the people who don't want you together."

Nicole's throat ached. She blinked back tears, staring out the window at the dark horizon. The ocean roared steadily, endlessly, like it didn't care whose hearts it swallowed.

She tightened her grip on Paige's hand, holding on because it was all she could do.

And she knew Paige was right.

Love was one thing. Families were another. Families who hated your loved one could destroy any chance you have at happiness.

"I don't know. I can't answer that—not yet. I need to understand how they did this to us, and whether we can ever get past it. Right now, everything is up in the air, and it has to stay there until this trial is over. A trial about a young woman who wasn't accepted into a wealthy family. Do you see? It's not just her life on trial in that courtroom. It feels like mine is too."

And sometimes, families were the most dangerous force of all. Bianca's trial proved it—an unflinching reminder of what happened when love collided with pride and money, when bloodlines mattered more than the beating heart of the person beside you. Every testimony, every exhibit pulled Nicole deeper into the sickening thought that she might be prosecuting the wrong person.

The evidence pointed one way, but her instincts...her instincts whispered another. And the weight of that nearly broke her. She hated being wrong. Hated the idea that her drive for justice might be blinding her. Because if she was wrong, then Bianca and her baby weren't just victims of a single man's crime, they were casualties of a family's ruthless refusal to accept her. And that truth was harder to face than any jury.

Only her first chair knew that Tripp had sent over new evidence. Evidence that drew suspicion to another person.

Soon the others drifted off to bed, and Nicole slipped out onto the deck, her glass still half-full. The boards creaked under her bare feet, the night air warm and salt-sweet. Out beyond the railing, the ocean stretched into darkness, its rhythm steady, endless, indifferent.

She tipped her glass, watching the moonlight ripple across the wine, and let out a long breath.

Paige's words clung like sea spray on her skin: *Not whether you and Tripp still love each other. But whether you could survive the people who don't want you together.*

Nicole closed her eyes, her throat thick. She'd spent years burying it, denying it, convincing herself she had moved on. But here, under the sweep of stars and the roar of the tide, there was no hiding.

She still loved him.

The truth sat in her chest, heavy and certain, terrifying in its simplicity.

She lifted the glass to her lips, drained the last swallow, and stared into the dark horizon. On Monday, she'd be the prosecutor again, sharp, steady, unshakable.

But tonight, alone with the sea, she let herself admit it. God, she still loved Tripp Masterson. Now, the question that remained was whether she could accept his mother. And would her family accept Tripp? Or did he and she move somewhere no one knew them and start fresh?

CHAPTER 15

Nicole rose from her chair, smoothing her jacket with practiced precision. She could feel the press of a hundred eyes on her, the jury box waiting, the gallery buzzing faintly with anticipation. Even Judge Price shifted forward on the bench, sensing this testimony would matter.

Her pulse drummed beneath her ribs, but her voice came steady, measured. She had to keep it that way. No matter what storm raged inside, the jury could never see her falter.

The lead investigator had testified days ago, laying out the facts as he saw them. But this man was different. He wasn't here to recap the scene—he was a weapons expert, and Nicole knew his testimony carried a weight that could tip the scales of the entire trial. The jury would hang on his words. And so would she.

As he walked to the stand, Nicole's pulse quickened.

Her fingers tightened around the pen in her hand until it bit into her skin, grounding her. She forced her shoulders back, spine straight, though tension coiled in her stomach like a live wire.

This moment mattered. The wrong question, the wrong tone, could unravel everything she'd built.

When he raised his hand to take the oath, Nicole exhaled slowly, as though releasing every doubt with that breath. Stay steady. Stay sharp. This is the turning point.

"Mr. Daniels," she began, "please remind the jury of your credentials."

The weapons specialist sat tall, a man used to being listened to. "I'm a forensic firearms examiner with the state crime lab. I've been working in ballistics for twenty-two years. I've testified in over a hundred cases."

"Thank you." Nicole angled her body toward the jury, her hands loose at her sides, every movement designed to project calm authority. "You examined the firearm recovered in this case?"

"Yes, ma'am."

"Tell us what you found."

Daniels adjusted his glasses, opened his folder, and launched into his report. "The weapon was a .38 caliber revolver. Classic design. Well-maintained. Recently fired. The fatal bullet recovered from the victim's body was conclusively matched to this revolver. There's no doubt it's the murder weapon."

A murmur rolled through the gallery. Nicole let the silence stretch, then tilted her head, her voice smooth. "Mr.

Daniels, when a firearm is logged into evidence, ownership records are traced, are they not?"

"Yes."

"And did you trace this weapon?"

"I did."

Nicole paused. She could feel the moment building like a storm cell gathering in the humid summer sky. She glanced at the jury, letting her gaze move slowly from face to face. She wanted them leaning in before she asked.

"And to whom was this firearm registered?"

Daniels checked his notes, though he didn't need to. His voice was crisp, certain. "Mrs. Evelyn Reddick."

The gallery erupted. Whispers, gasps, the scrape of chairs shifting.

Nicole's pulse spiked, but outwardly she didn't move. She had known the answer the moment she saw the report, and worried how the jury would react to that information. And justly so.

Judge Price's gavel cracked like thunder. "Order! I will have order in this courtroom!"

Tripp was on his feet before she could ask her next question. "Objection, Your Honor." His voice rang sharp across the room. "May we approach the bench?"

Judge Price's brows lifted, but he gave a curt nod. "Counsel, approach."

Nicole gathered her notes, then joined Tripp at the bench.

The low hum of the white-noise machine filled the

courtroom as Nicole and Tripp stepped up to the bench. Judge Price leaned forward, eyes sharp.

"All right, counsel," he said in a low growl. "What exactly is going on here? Why is this jury hearing that the murder weapon belongs to someone other than the defendant?"

Nicole spoke first, her voice cool but edged with steel. "It doesn't matter whose name is on the paperwork. What matters is who kept the gun in that closet, who had the key, who had control. And that was Derrick Reddick. The state arrested him on that basis."

Tripp braced his hands against the bench, meeting the judge's gaze. "With respect, Your Honor, the state's case hinges on tying this gun to my client — and we've just heard it's not his. That fact goes directly to reasonable doubt."

Judge Price shifted his gaze back to Nicole. "Ms. Reyes, why didn't the police pursue Mrs. Reddick if the gun was hers?"

Nicole sighed and wondered if they had gone after the wrong person. "Because the totality of the evidence pointed to Derrick. He had a documented argument with the victim the night before. Witnesses placed him at her house. He had scratches on his hands consistent with a struggle. Add the firearm found in his possession, that's more than probable cause for an arrest."

Tripp cut in, his tone sharp. "But fingerprints don't lie, Your Honor. Derrick's prints weren't on that gun. It was wiped clean."

Nicole's voice rose, tight with control. "A wiped weapon is consistent with consciousness of guilt. The most logical person to clean it would be the person in possession — Derrick Reddick."

Tripp narrowed his eyes. "Or it proves the state has been looking at the wrong Reddick all along."

The judge rapped his knuckles against the bench, the sound sharp even over the hum.

"Enough. This isn't the time for speeches. The evidence about ownership and prints is admissible; the jury will hear it. What weight they give it is their job, not mine."

Nicole inclined her head. "Understood, Your Honor."

Tripp gave a clipped nod, but his eyes burned. "Then let the record reflect, Your Honor, that nothing we've heard proves my client ever pulled that trigger."

Judge Price's mouth twitched, almost a grimace. "The record will reflect it. Now get back to your tables and keep this trial on track."

The white noise clicked off. The two of them stepped back, masks sliding into place as though nothing had happened.

But Nicole caught the flicker in Tripp's eyes. She turned back toward the jury box, pulse still racing.

Behind her, Tripp exhaled slowly. He was defending his client with skill. But she couldn't shake the question now buzzing in her own mind:

Was he also defending his mother?

From the corner of her eye, Nicole saw Evelyn Reddick in the gallery, seated as regally as if she were hosting a luncheon. Her pearls gleamed under the lights, her expression calm, controlled.

It was like staring at Tripp's mother all over again. The same cold disdain. The same hunger for control. Different woman, same poison. And that's when it hit her hard. Had Derrick really killed Bianca or had his mother?

Why did it feel like the woman had more to gain from Bianca's death?

Nicole turned back to the stand. "Mr. Daniels, where did the police find the pistol?"

"In Derrick Reddick's apartment."

Nicole's throat felt tight. "Was it secured?"

Daniels nodded. "In a locked case."

The gallery buzzed louder, a low hum of shock.

Tripp shot to his feet. "Objection, Your Honor! The state is insinuating, without foundation, that Mrs. Reddick is implicated in this crime. She is not on trial here."

Nicole pivoted toward the bench, keeping her voice calm though adrenaline surged through her veins. "Your Honor, this is directly relevant to possession and access — the jury is entitled to hear it."

Judge Price rapped his gavel again. "The objection is noted. The witness's answer will stand. The jury will consider it for what it's worth."

Nicole inclined her head. "Thank you, Your Honor." She turned back.

She wanted to press further. To ask the questions clawing at her: Could Evelyn have been the killer? Why was her gun used? Or was this just a red herring to throw her? But strategy held her back. The answers would come, but not yet. Not today.

She drew herself up, her mask of composure flawless. "No further questions, Your Honor."

"Mr. Masterson, you may cross-examine the witness."

As she walked back to her table, her legs felt unsteady beneath her. She sat, clasped her hands on the desk, and forced her breathing into rhythm.

Inside, though, her mind spun.

Her gaze flicked across the courtroom to Tripp. He was staring at her, his eyes dark, unreadable. But she knew him well enough to recognize the storm gathering behind them.

All the signs had pointed to Derrick Reddick, not his mother, and yet suddenly she was having doubts. And she'd latched onto Derrick being the killer and had not properly vetted his mother, because the woman didn't appear to have opportunity. Derrick did.

Nicole's throat tightened. This case wasn't just about Bianca anymore. It was about patterns. Families who thought they could control their lives. Mothers who decided whose love was acceptable and whose was disposable.

She forced herself to sit straighter, to face forward. The jury couldn't see her doubt. They had to see her as steady, unshaken.

But inside, she knew the trial had just changed course.

And Evelyn Reddick's perfect mask was starting to crack. Had she killed Bianca?

CHAPTER 16

The words still reverberated through the courtroom like a gunshot.

The firearm was registered to Mrs. Evelyn Reddick.

Derrick's mother.

Tripp rose slowly, smoothing his jacket, every motion deliberate. He couldn't afford a flicker of hesitation, not here, not in front of twelve jurors staring at him with wide eyes, waiting to see if the revelation had absolved his case.

He glanced once at the gallery. Evelyn Reddick sat rigid, pearls gleaming at her throat, expression fixed in icy composure. To anyone else, she appeared to be a society matron enduring an inconvenience. But Tripp saw what others might miss: a hard glint in her eyes, the subtle lift of her chin.

Control. Denial. Power dressed in silk.

She reminded him so much of his own mother that it scraped raw against old wounds.

Was it possible?

Could she have done to her son what Tripp's mother had done to him and Nicole?

He forced the thought down and approached the witness stand. His voice, when it came, was calm and precise.

"Mr. Daniels, you testified this firearm was a .38 revolver, correct?"

"Yes, sir."

"This type of revolver, is it rare?"

Daniels adjusted his glasses. "No. Fairly standard. There are thousands in circulation."

Tripp nodded. He wanted the jury to hear that word, *thousands.* He paced slowly, letting it sink in before continuing.

"And when you examined this weapon for fingerprints, you found the gun had been wiped clean."

"Yes, sir," the man said.

"How could you tell it had been wiped clean?"

"There was gun cleaning residue left on the wooden grip of the thirty-eight."

"It's possible anyone could have had access to that weapon and fired it that night."

"Whoever had access to the suspect's home, yes."

Tripp turned slightly, letting the jury see his face. Calm. Controlled. "So while the registration showed the weapon was purchased by Mrs. Reddick fifteen years ago, it was found in her son's possession."

"Yes."

He gave a slight nod, then stepped back. "So to be absolutely clear: you cannot tell this jury who fired that weapon on the night Bianca Laurent was killed."

"No, sir."

"And you cannot tell this jury when Mrs. Reddick last touched it."

"No, sir."

"Thank you. No further questions."

Tripp returned to the defense table, each step measured, every muscle coiled tightly. He lowered himself into his chair, keeping his face carefully blank.

But his chest burned.

Because Evelyn Reddick's mask, cold, perfect, untouchable, had cracked for just a second when her name had been tied to the weapon. And Tripp knew that look. He'd seen it in his own mother's eyes whenever she was cornered.

He forced his gaze back to Derrick, who was pale, eyes darting between his attorney and his mother. Panic radiated off him. Tripp leaned closer, murmuring low so only his client could hear.

"Stay calm. We've just planted reasonable doubt."

Derrick swallowed hard, nodding. But the young man's gaze slid back to Evelyn, and Tripp knew doubt had started to creep in for him too.

The judge cleared his throat, breaking the tension. "The witness may step down."

Daniels rose, gathering his notes, oblivious to the storm he'd left behind.

Tripp straightened his papers, keeping his hands steady even as his mind spun. He had done his job, shifted the jury's focus, reminded them that the evidence was circumstantial, and planted the idea that Derrick wasn't the only possible suspect.

But the sight of Evelyn sitting there, unflinching, still gnawed at him.

Because while he had defended Derrick with skill, he couldn't shake the thought that maybe the real danger wasn't at the prosecution table at all.

Maybe it was sitting in the gallery, wearing pearls and a smile sharp enough to cut glass.

It was time to have a serious discussion with his client. Just as soon as they had a recess.

"Ladies and gentlemen of the jury, we're going to conclude for today. Remember my admonishments: do not discuss the case with anyone, do not allow anyone to discuss it in your presence, and do not consume any media coverage related to the case. We'll resume tomorrow morning at nine a.m. Court is adjourned."

As soon as the judge banged his gavel, Tripp turned toward his client. They needed to talk now.

The courtroom hummed with low whispers as the jury filed out in a ripple of dark suits and wary eyes.

Tripp sat rigid at the defense table, his pen motionless above his legal pad. He'd defused what he could in cross, but the echo of those words still thundered in his chest.

The murder weapon was registered to Evelyn Reddick. He'd known that since he took over the case, but it wasn't until he sat here in the courtroom, surrounded by silence, scrutiny, and the weight of what was at stake, that the truth hit him like a punch to the gut.

He'd convinced himself she'd given her son the gun to protect him, to keep him safe. But what if that wasn't it at all? What if she hadn't handed it over... but had been hiding it? What if she never meant for anyone to find it?

But that didn't make sense.

The police were going to accuse Derrick, because he was the boyfriend, the text messages, and the fight they'd had. Why would she put her son at risk?

Beside him, Derrick leaned forward, his voice a low hiss. "What the hell was that? They're going after my mother now?" His eyes were wide, panicked. "She didn't do this, Tripp. She couldn't have."

Tripp kept his expression steady, his voice low. "Listen to me. All that matters right now is the jury. They just heard there's another possible suspect. That helps us. It doesn't convict her. It creates *doubt*. And that's what we need."

"But why her?" Derrick's hands shook on the table. "Why even drag her into this? The gun was mine. She gave me the gun when I moved out. That's why it was in my closet."

Tripp's head snapped toward him. "She gave it to you?"

Derrick swallowed hard. "Yeah. Said it was for protection. I never even loaded it, I swear. I didn't think she—" He stopped, shaking his head. "She's not a killer."

"Does she have a key to your apartment?"

Derrick's face went white, and he coughed. "Yes."

Tripp's jaw tightened. He'd heard that tone before, the blind insistence of a son unwilling to see what his mother might be capable of. His gut churned, memories clawing their way up.

Nicole. That sundress. His mother's lies.

Before he could respond, movement in the gallery caught his eye. Evelyn herself was rising, sweeping past the curious stares like a queen moving through her court. She paused at the bar, waiting, every inch of her composed, immaculate.

"Son, I need a word with your lawyer. You're going to beat this. I just know it," she said with a smile that felt cold to Tripp.

The young man got up and walked out of the courtroom.

"Mr. Masterson," she said.

Tripp ground his teeth. The last thing he wanted was a confrontation with a woman who mirrored every cold instinct he'd grown up with. But refusing her here, now, would only create more whispers. He rose, buttoned his jacket, and followed her out into the marble hallway.

The air was cooler out there, quieter, but still heavy with tension. Evelyn turned to him, her posture flawless, her perfume a cloying mix of roses and steel.

"You allowed them to drag my name through the mud," she said, her voice low but seething.

Tripp held her gaze, his own voice clipped. "I didn't allow anything. The evidence speaks for itself. Your son is on trial. I'm defending him. Your name is on the register for the gun. Your son is my only concern."

Her eyes flashed. "My son is innocent."

"Then this evidence shouldn't concern you. It shows that there could be more than one suspect. Anyone who knew about that gun in Derrick's closet is now a suspect."

A pause. Just long enough for the lie to glitter between them.

Evelyn stepped closer, lowering her voice. "You're clever, Mr. Masterson. Clever enough to know how dangerous this line of questioning is. The prosecution is trying to use this to destroy my son. He will do everything in his power to protect me, and that means even admitting to this murder to save me. Don't let him."

Tripp studied her, the mask she wore so carefully. He thought of the jury's faces when they heard her name tied to the weapon. Some had leaned forward, hungry. Others had gone pale. Evelyn was right about one thing: her presence in the case had changed the tide.

And then, like a match struck in the dark, the thought came.

If Evelyn Reddick truly believed she had nothing to hide...then put her on the stand.

Tripp's pulse steadied, a dangerous kind of calm washing over him. It was a gamble. A huge one. But it might also be the only way to show the jury she wasn't the shooter or, if she slipped, to expose the truth once and for all.

He let the silence stretch before speaking. "If you want

the jury to see you as blameless, Mrs. Reddick, then you'll have to tell them yourself."

Her eyes narrowed. "You mean testify?"

"Yes." His voice was measured, but inside, something twisted. "You take the stand. You explain why the gun was in Derrick's possession, and you do it calmly, credibly, so the jury sees this for what it is, a red herring."

Evelyn's lips pressed into a thin line. For a flicker of a moment, her composure cracked. "I do not belong on that witness stand."

"Then we let the jury imagine what you're hiding and believe that your son fired the weapon."

She bristled, then glanced away, her gaze sweeping over the polished floor as if she could find another path. When she looked back, her mask was in place again. "If that's what it takes to protect my son, then I'll do it."

Tripp gave a single nod, though his gut twisted harder. Putting her on the stand could either save Derrick...or destroy him.

He turned back toward the courtroom doors, his thoughts a storm. Nicole would shred Evelyn on cross if she sensed blood in the water. And God help him, he wasn't entirely sure Evelyn wouldn't bleed.

As he reached for the door handle, Derrick walked up beside him, his voice desperate and shaky: "She didn't do it, Tripp. Tell me you don't think my mom could do this."

Tripp closed his eyes for a beat, jaw tight. *She reminds me of my own mother,* he thought grimly. *And I know exactly what women like that are capable of.*

When his eyes opened again, he let out a slow breath. The gamble was set.

"Derrick, get some rest. Tomorrow could be a rough day."

The prosecution should rest tomorrow. Then he would tell Derrick the plan.

They were calling Evelyn Reddick to the stand.

CHAPTER 17

The night was still except for the chorus of cicadas and the slow slap of water against the pilings. Nicole sat curled in the deck chair, the summer breeze cooling her and protecting her from mosquitoes. A lightweight throw rested on her shoulders. A single lamp glowed behind her in the kitchen, spilling a sliver of light across the wooden planks, but beyond that, everything was swallowed in moonlight and shadow.

The tide rolled in and out like a heartbeat, steady and unyielding, a sharp contrast to the storm inside her.

All her life, her parents' house had clung to the edge of the ocean, her father's boat tied faithfully to the pilings out back. That boat had been part of the view, part of the rhythm of her childhood, but now it was gone. Some days, she wondered why they still lived here at all. And yet, she couldn't deny she loved the sound of the surf, the steady hush of waves brushing against the shore, comforting, almost like a heartbeat.

Except when storms rolled in. Then the water rose angry and wild, slamming against the wood, shaking the house with every crash. On those nights, fear sat heavy in her chest, the same fear curling through her now. Her case felt like it was slipping through her fingers, its foundation washing out from under her. For the first time, she doubted the story she'd built, doubted that Derrick Reddick had pulled the trigger that killed Bianca.

The trial replayed in her mind like a film she couldn't turn off. The jurors' shifting eyes, the way Evelyn Reddick had sat in the gallery with her chin high, the weight of the evidence balanced on the edge of a knife.

What unsettled her most wasn't just the woman herself, but how closely she resembled Tripp's mother, the same poise, the same calculating eyes, the same chill that could cut straight through you.

Tomorrow, the state would rest. Nicole would have to rise, thank the jury for their patience, and yield the floor to Tripp. Then it would be his turn, to dismantle her case and convince the jury his client was innocent.

The thought made her stomach twist. She knew how good he was. She'd watched him in court enough to recognize the precision of his cross-examinations, the way he built a narrative until it seemed inevitable. And this time, he'd be wielding his skill like a blade aimed at her.

Staring into the dark horizon, she analyzed each piece of evidence. Did they have the right person on trial? No matter how much she tried to keep the lines clean, prosecutor, defense counsel, adversaries, she couldn't. Not with Tripp. Not when every word they spoke seemed to stir embers she'd spent half a lifetime trying to smother.

And seeing him every day reawakened every hidden ache in her body parts of her that still longed for him, still wanted him, still needed him like air.

The screen door creaked. Nicole glanced back as her mother stepped out, moving slowly, a mug of tea in her hand. She wore her robe and slippers, her sweater draped around her shoulders like a shawl.

"You're still awake," her mother said softly.

Nicole forced a smile. "Couldn't sleep."

Her mother settled into the chair beside her, setting the mug carefully on the armrest. For a long while, they sat together, listening to the hum of insects and the whisper of waves.

Finally, her mother said, "I know you're upset. But you need to understand something. Your father and I were only trying to keep you from making a big mistake."

Nicole's chest tightened. She turned, the blanket slipping down her arm. "A mistake?"

Her mother didn't look at her. She stared into the night as though the answer were out there in the dark. "You were seventeen, Nicole. You had your whole life ahead of you. And Tripp...he wasn't..." She drew a breath. "He wasn't the right one for you."

Nicole let out a sharp laugh, bitter and raw. "The right one? He was the *only* one. Don't you get it? I have loved him since the moment I first saw him." Her voice cracked on the words, but she pushed on. "No one else has ever made me feel the way he does. Not before. Not since. Not ever."

She'd grown up with parents who paraded their love like it was a crown, yet when it came to hers, they gutted it without remorse. They weren't blind—they knew exactly what she had with Tripp, and they carved it out of her life with surgical precision, leaving her bleeding. And for that, she could never forgive them.

They hadn't protected her—they'd destroyed her.

Her mother's face flickered, guilt surfacing before she smoothed it away.

"We only wanted to protect you. You were so young. He came from a family...well, you know what his mother was like. Ambitious. Ruthless. We thought—"

"You thought what?" Nicole cut in, her voice rising. "That I wasn't strong enough? That I couldn't make my own choices? That I didn't know my own heart? That Tripp wouldn't protect me from his family?"

"You were a kid," her mother said, sharper now. "And I didn't trust that boy to protect you."

The statement cut deep, sharp as a stake through her heart. Would he really have protected her back then? Could he have stood against his family for her? She wanted to believe he would have—but doubt gnawed at her. Had he been strong enough then...was he even strong enough now?

Sadly, they'd been robbed of the chance to find out—

robbed of knowing whether their love could have survived the crushing weight of family, the demands of school, and the vows of marriage. That loss gnawed at her, a wound that would never fully close.

"I was in love," Nicole shot back. "And you destroyed that. You, Dad, and his mother all decided what was best for us, and we had no say. What if your mother had done that to you and Dad?"

Her mother flinched, looking down at her lap. "We thought we were saving you from a life of regret. You had college, law school, a career ahead of you. We didn't want you tied down before you'd even begun."

Nicole's throat burned. "And what did that buy me, Mom? Do you know what it's like to go through relationship after relationship and feel nothing? To sit across from men who look good on paper and feel absolutely empty because none of them are him? Because the only person who ever saw me, really saw me, was the boy you helped tear away from me?"

Her mother's eyes glistened in the moonlight, but she didn't speak.

Nicole drew a ragged breath, her voice breaking. "How will you and Dad react if we get back together?"

The question hung heavy in the night air.

Her mother looked at her then, really looked, as though she were searching for the little girl she'd once raised. The silence stretched, the weight of years pressing down between them.

Nicole's chest ached, her heart pounding in her ears. She wanted an answer. She needed an answer.

But her mother didn't give one.

Instead, she rose slowly, gathering her robe around her, her tea still untouched on the armrest. She rested a hand on Nicole's shoulder, just briefly, a fleeting touch of warmth that felt like both comfort and apology.

Her voice was quiet, almost tender. "Some loves aren't meant to be easy."

And with that, she turned and slipped back inside, the screen door closing with a soft thud.

Nicole sat frozen, her throat tight, her mother's words echoing in her head.

Some loves aren't meant to be easy.

She pulled the blanket tighter around her shoulders, staring into the endlessly dark horizon. The ocean kept its rhythm, steady and uncaring.

She'd always thought love should be about choice. About two people who wanted each other enough to fight.

But tonight, alone on the deck, she realized love was also about survival.

And no matter what her parents thought, no matter what his mother thought, she wasn't sure she could survive losing Tripp Masterson a second time. She wasn't even sure they could survive their parents a second time.

CHAPTER 18

Saturday was moving day. But tonight, his mother had asked him to be home for dinner. Why? he had no idea, but he would use the opportunity to tell her he had another place to live. His own place.

His mother's dining room gleamed as though it had been frozen in amber since his childhood. The chandelier cast its steady glow, the table polished to perfection, the lilies in the vase stiff and white as bone.

Everything in its place. Everything under control. Except for his feelings, which were raw.

"Marianne called me this morning," his mother said, her voice smooth as she speared a delicate bite of salmon. "She enjoyed dinner very much. She said she thought you were... charming."

Marianne, that was the name of the blonde his mother had paraded around, a woman with all the personality of wet cardboard. She must've been the so-called "appropriate" match his mother had thrown in Nicole's face. Not happening. Tripp clenched his jaw, every muscle tight with the urge to confront his mother, to call her out for every lie, every manipulation.

But not yet.

Not until this trial was finished. That reckoning would come, and when it did, he'd make damn sure she never had the power to rip Nicole out of his life again. Trust was fragile, and his mother had already smashed theirs to pieces once. He'd be damned if she destroyed it a second time.

Next time, she wouldn't see him as her obedient son; she'd see him as her reckoning.

Tripp cut his steak with slow precision, his jaw tight. "I'm sure she did. You made sure of it."

Her eyes flicked up, bright and sharp. "What's that supposed to mean?"

"It means," Tripp said evenly, "that you've been arranging my social calendar without my consent. Again. I'm not interested in Marianne."

She wouldn't listen to reason. She never had. She'd keep scheming, pushing, clawing for control until she got what she wanted. Unless he shut her down now, brutally and decisively, she'd never stop.

Her mouth curved, a smile that didn't reach her eyes. "You're too busy to do it yourself. And really, Dustin, it's not a crime for a mother to want her son settled with the right kind of woman."

This time, he wouldn't bend, he'd break her hold, even if it meant burning every bridge between them.

He set his fork down, folding his napkin with deliberate care. "I'm not calling her. I'm not seeing her again. The answer is no. Bring her around, and I promise to embarrass you."

His mother loathed embarrassment, despised humiliation. If this didn't bring her to heel, nothing ever would.

A flicker of irritation crossed her perfectly painted features. "She's from an excellent family. Educated, gracious, poised. You could do much worse. She's exactly the type of woman you need."

Her persistence was relentless, corrosive, and if she didn't back off, it would destroy what little remained between them. Especially if she dared to stand against Nicole. He wouldn't let her sabotage them again. Not this time.

"A brainless, conservative, blonde is your idea of the perfect woman for me? You don't know me very well, Mother. I could do much better," Tripp said softly, leaning back in his chair.

She gave a sharp little laugh, brittle as glass. "Better? You mean Nicole Reyes?"

The name landed between them like a curse.

"Yes," Tripp said. He didn't flinch.

Her knife clattered against her plate. "You can't be serious."

"I've never been more serious." He leaned forward, his

elbows braced on the table. "Tell me something, Mother. How would you react if I got back together with her?"

His mother froze, silver poised in her hand, before she set it down with slow, deliberate grace. Her voice, when it came, was venom wrapped in silk. "Nicole Reyes was a mistake. She nearly derailed your future once, and she will do it again if you let her. That girl was nothing but a ladder-climber. A nobody. My son needs someone to help him reach the next level. Someone with a pedigree. Someone with connections."

"For what?"

"Judge? Senator? President," she said.

Tripp lowered his elbows off the table and resisted the urge to clench his fists, but his voice stayed calm. "Not happening. Nicole was everything. She is everything. And I was a fool to let you convince me otherwise."

Where she'd ever gotten the notion he wanted a career in politics, he had no idea. What mattered now was that she faced the truth, owned what she'd done to him and Nicole, and made a choice. Either accept Nicole, or resign herself to becoming an old, bitter, lonely woman.

Her eyes flashed, cold and hard. "I convinced you of nothing. You came to your senses. You realized what kind of girl she was, grasping, needy, willing to trap you if you were too blind to see it."

The woman was delusional, her memory dulled by time and twisted to fit her own version of the truth. The reality was far different—he'd been abandoned on his college doorstep, a hollowed-out shell, a broken young man left to pick apart the ruins of what had happened, desperate to understand why his world had been ripped away.

The words sliced at old wounds, but Tripp didn't let them show. "You can repeat your script all you want, Mother. It doesn't change the truth. I loved her then. I love her now."

Her composure cracked, the guise slipping to reveal the woman beneath. Her voice turned sharp, vulgar. "Love?" She spat out the word as if it were filth. "Don't talk to me about love. Love is weakness. Love ruins men. What lasts is money, family, and the name you pass on to others. Do you really think that girl could carry our name with dignity? She's trash, Tripp. She always was. And her family…really, son. Gutter trash."

For a long moment, he just stared at her. He saw not the elegant society matron she wanted the world to see, but the truth beneath it: a woman who had built her life on control, who would poison anyone who threatened her grip on it.

"What happened to make you so cruel?"

She didn't respond.

Slowly, he rose, pushing back his chair. His voice was steady and low, yet it carried. "Then you don't want me around any longer."

Her head snapped up. "What did you say?"

He leaned across the table, holding her gaze without flinching. "Because when Nicole and I get back together, and we will, we are not going to let family destroy us a second time."

The chandelier hummed faintly overhead. Neither of them moved.

Finally, his mother scoffed, lifting her glass of wine as though dismissing him.

"You're a fool, Dustin. Mark my words: that girl will be the end of you. Don't expect me at your wedding. The birth of your first child or anything else. In fact, don't think I won't sell the law firm."

Threats. More and more threats. He'd had enough. Time for it to end.

"All my life, you've been threatening me if I don't do things your way." Tripp straightened, adjusting his jacket. "Do it. Sell the firm. At least, I'll finally be living my own life without your threats."

He turned, walked across the polished floor, and left her sitting alone at her perfect table.

For the first time in twenty years, he didn't look back. It felt good to call out her threats. After the trial, he'd see about his own law firm, one with Nicole.

"By the way, I'm moving out Saturday," he said.

He heard her wine glass hit the floor. Damn, she was mad. Good.

Like any son, he loved his mother, but he loved Nicole more. Seeing her again, all the old feelings had returned like a tsunami crashing toward shore.

When this trial was over, they were going to be together. He expected the trial to end tomorrow, when he introduced new evidence. Evidence that had been right in front of him all along. Evidence that would spin this trial on its head.

Time to be a good lawyer, and then he could have Nicole back.

Nicole rose this morning with grit in her veins and a knot under her breastbone that refused to loosen. She'd known hard mornings, after heartbreak, after betrayal, after the kind of sleepless nights that left salt behind her eyes, but this one carried a different weight.

The conversation with Tripp still vibrated under her skin, a live wire she couldn't ground. His voice, his conviction, the heat that had once been theirs, old embers flared as unwelcome light on everything she needed to keep in shadow.

Not here. Not now.

She smoothed her jacket, lifted her chin, and stepped into the arena of polished wood and fluorescent truth.

After the judge and jury were seated, she rose.

"Your honor, the prosecution rests." She made herself sound steady, as if the past hadn't just brushed the inside of her ribcage with cold fingers.

Judge Price nodded. The bailiff called the room to order. And then Tripp stood.

"Your honor, the defense calls Mrs. Evelyn Reddick."

A ripple passed through the gallery. Heads turned. Pens poised. Even the jurors shifted forward as a single, attentive organism.

Nicole leaped to her feet. "Objection, Your Honor. Mrs. Reddick was not included on the defense's witness list."

The defense attorney rose. "Your Honor, new evidence came to light late yesterday, and the prosecution was provided a copy as soon as we received it."

The judge raised a brow. "Is that true, Miss Reyes?"

Nicole hesitated. "Yes, Your Honor. We did receive the evidence last night, but we haven't had adequate time to review it."

The judge considered for a moment, then spoke firmly. "I'll allow the witness, for now. But I'll be watching closely. If this turns into a fishing expedition, I won't hesitate to strike the testimony. Proceed."

Derrick's mother rose with the unhurried grace of a woman who'd always been obeyed. Cream suit, pearls, hair sculpted to perfection, Evelyn looked like she'd been poured into power and polished until she gleamed. She walked the aisle as if approaching a stage, not a witness box.

She looked like Mrs. America, her crown gleaming as much a weapon as it was armor.

Nicole felt the room's temperature drop a degree. Everything about Evelyn was beautiful and brittle, like something expensive that could cut you if you touched it wrong.

The oath was administered; Evelyn's manicured hand rested on the Bible as if it were an accessory rather than a sacrament. She sat, back straight, mouth serene.

Tripp approached with a soft smile and an even softer voice, silk laid over steel. "Mrs. Reddick, you are the defendant's mother?"

"Yes." The confidence of generations rode on that single syllable.

"And his father?"

"His father died when he was twelve," she responded.

He let the quiet bloom, gave the jury time to map Evelyn's composure onto their own expectations: a mother defending her son, a matriarch anchoring her family. Nicole recognized the move. She'd used it herself. But she also recognized the slight tightness around Evelyn's mouth.

"How did you feel," Tripp asked, "when you learned your son's girlfriend, Bianca Laurent, was pregnant?"

Nicole's gaze drilled into the woman, desperate for even the faintest crack in her polished armor. How could she have been so blind? She should have suspected her from the very beginning. Instead, she'd let the evidence lull her, let her own scars from dealing with women like Evelyn Reddick twist her judgment. And now the truth mocked her, she'd failed to see what had been staring her in the face all along.

Evelyn blinked once, lashes like tiny fans. "Surprised. Concerned."

"Concerned for whom?"

"My son. His future. Derrick has ambitions."

Ambitions. The word had been a blade in Nicole's life once, wielded in a dim parlor by a different mother with the same smile. *He has a future, dear.* The memory skittered under her skin like a moth against glass.

How could she have forgotten? That day Mrs. Masterson summoned her to the house, her voice like ice as she delivered the ultimatum: *Leave my son alone, or you'll regret the day you met him.* The threat had seared itself into her bones. And yet somehow, Nicole had buried it, shoved it so deep, she'd almost convinced herself it hadn't happened. How could she have pushed that memory out of her mind?

The check she'd slid across the table, payment to disappear, dressed up as help for her college expenses. Nicole remembered staring at it, her hands shaking, her pride warring with her rage. She'd pushed it back across the polished wood, refusing to be bought like some cheap transaction. The humiliation burned hotter than fire as she stormed out of that ice palace, sick with disgust and betrayal.

"And did you share those concerns with him?" Tripp's tone stayed gentle.

"Of course. I told him he had worked too hard to be derailed."

"By Bianca?"

"By circumstance," Evelyn said, correcting him with a velvet edge.

Nicole's pen dug into her palm. *Circumstance.* That was the word women like Evelyn used to measure other people's worth. You were either born into money and pedigree, or you were one of the faceless masses.

Tripp continued. "Mrs. Reddick, did you ever speak to your son about Bianca's suitability as a wife?"

Evelyn's jaw feathered. "I may have suggested she wasn't compatible with him long-term."

A hum, low as a hive, moved through the jurors. Tripp's eyes sharpened.

"And the pregnancy?" he asked. "Did you advise your son how to handle it?"

"I told him options existed," Evelyn said, pearls winking beneath the lights. "That he didn't have to let one mistake dictate his entire life."

That meeting with Mrs. Masterson hadn't been about polite concern, it had been a warning. Don't get pregnant. Don't you dare try to trap my son. The accusation had seared through Nicole like acid, her fury rising at the audacity of it. She and Tripp had made their own vow, a sacred promise not to have children until school was behind them.

And yet his mother, in all her arrogance, had assumed Nicole was nothing more than a schemer lying in wait to snare him just like Evelyn Reddick had assumed about Bianca.

"Options," Tripp repeated. "Including abortion."

"Yes." The word snapped like a twig. "Bianca had her own plans. Law school. A career. She wasn't prepared to support Derrick's path. She would have ruined him."

The air thinned. Nicole's chest tightened. History repeating itself.

Tripp's voice lost its velvet. "So to be clear, you told your son that Bianca was unsuitable. That her pregnancy was a mistake. That the child she carried was not worth altering his plans for."

Evelyn's composure flickered, then settled. "I told him his future was too important to be tied down by a girl who didn't belong in our family."

Nicole swallowed hard. It was always the same song: our family, our kind, our future. A hymn to exclusion, sung in perfect pitch.

Tripp took a breath, changed lanes. "Where were you on the night Ms. Laurent was killed?"

Evelyn smiled. It didn't reach her eyes. "At home. Reading."

"Alone?"

"Yes. Derrick was out with friends, not that he still lives at home. But I had no plans."

Tripp nodded, turning a page in his binder. "Phone records show a call from your number to Ms. Laurent at 9:35 p.m. that night. What was discussed?"

"I urged her to terminate the pregnancy," Evelyn said, voice cool. "To let Derrick finish his studies. He's going to be a doctor." A quick, maternal glance toward her son, softening like sunlight, well-practiced and deadly.

Nicole had seen that look on Mrs. Masterson's face before.

"And what did Bianca say?"

"She refused. Her family is Catholic. She was not terminating the pregnancy."

"Did you threaten her?"

Evelyn's smile sharpened. "I don't threaten. I reason."

A murmur spread from the back row. Nicole kept her face still. She understood what Tripp was doing.

Why had she been so blind? Because this wasn't new, she knew this kind of truth, had lived it, and it had carved scars deep into her. It was the kind of truth that stole your breath, that left you staring at the ceiling at three a.m., wondering how love could be twisted into something so cruel. And now, standing here, she felt it all over again—raw, merciless, and burning through her like fire.

Tripp walked a few steps, the rhythm of his soles on hardwood a metronome. "Mrs. Reddick, had you ever been to Ms. Laurent's home?"

"No."

"But you had her address."

"I'm sure it was in a file. Somewhere."

"Because you invited her to Derrick's graduation party?"

"Only because he insisted," Evelyn said, bored now. "Common courtesy."

"So you had her address," Tripp repeated, unblinking.

Evelyn's mouth went flat. "I suppose."

"Did you drive to her home that night?"

She gave a small, brittle laugh. "No."

Tripp lifted a single page, the paper whispering like a warning. "Let me direct your attention to Defense Exhibit A, a trip log from your vehicle's onboard computer. It shows your car leaving your residence at 10:03 p.m., stopping in front of Ms. Laurent's home at 10:27 p.m., and returning to your home at 11:51 p.m."

"Objection," Nicole snapped, not because she had a good reason, but rather that she didn't want Tripp to win, and clearly, he'd found their murderer. "Foundation. Authentication."

"Overruled, if you can lay it, Mr. Masterson," Judge Price said.

Tripp nodded. "Your Honor, these records were obtained via subpoena from the dealership's telematics service. The custodian of records authenticated them yesterday. The State received copies late last night."

Nicole had. She'd read them twice with growing unease. It all made sense now.

Evelyn's fingers tightened around the edge of the witness chair. "You had no right—"

"The timing," Tripp continued, "is ten minutes before Ms. Laurent's time of death, as established by the coroner's report already in evidence. Would you like to revise your testimony?"

"I did not kill her," Evelyn said. The smile was gone.

Tripp didn't blink. "You say you were at home reading. What book?"

She hesitated. "I was alone."

"Title?"

"I read many."

"Your home's security system shows your garage door opening at 10:01 p.m. and again at 11:53 p.m. Defense Exhibit B." He lifted another sheet. "The security company authenticated those as well."

A bead of sweat gathered at Evelyn's temple, delicate as dew. Nicole watched it fall and felt a bleak, awful satisfaction. Truth had its own gravity.

Tripp let the jury sit with the contradiction, then turned another page. "Mrs. Reddick, after Ms. Laurent was killed, the murder weapon, a .38 special, was discovered in your son's apartment. Are you familiar with the box in which it was stored?"

Her throat moved. "No."

He slid a glossy photograph onto the evidence cart. The projector splashed it onto the screen above the jury: the upscale foyer camera still, time-stamped 11:18 p.m., Evelyn entering Derrick's building in a dark pant suit, a rectangular manufacturer's box tucked against her side.

A collective inhale scraped the room.

"Do you deny this is you, Mrs. Reddick?"

Silence. A tiny tremor touched her hands.

"Do you deny that the box in your possession matches the serial-labeled container of the weapon later found in your son's apartment?"

She said nothing.

Tripp's voice dropped, intimate and lethal. "Mrs.

Reddick, did you carry the gun's box into your son's apartment the night Bianca Laurent was killed?"

"No!" She flinched and then, involuntarily, looked at Derrick. "Sweetheart, listen to me. I wasn't trying to frame you. You had an alibi. I was—" She swallowed. "I was trying to…put it somewhere safe."

Safe. Nicole's pen stilled. The word was a ricochet.

"Because you possessed it," Tripp said quietly. "Because you needed to hide it."

Evelyn's eyes flashed. "You're twisting—"

"Am I?" He moved one step closer, lowering his voice so the jury had to lean in. "Mrs. Reddick, Bianca refused your demand. She told you she would keep her baby. You told Derrick she was unsuitable. You told him to focus on his future, not hers. So you drove to her home, you confronted her, and when she resisted the version of your life for Derrick, you tried to impose—"

Evelyn's lips trembled. For a flicker, Nicole saw the girl Evelyn might once have been, frightened, furious, feral where no one could see. Then the façade snapped back.

"She was going to ruin him," Evelyn whispered.

Tripp didn't move. "Did you kill Bianca Laurent?"

The courtroom held its breath. Nicole's lungs burned. In her mind, she saw the parlor again, the check, the word options, the way it had felt to be weighed and found unsuitable. She thought of Bianca, young, brilliant, stubborn enough to want both a law degree and a life. She thought of Bianca's baby.

Evelyn's eyes hardened into diamonds. "That bitch was

going to ruin my son." The dam broke; the words poured out scalding. "She wanted to trap him, tie him down with her bastard, and drag him through the mud. I had to do something." She lifted her chin and unleashed the venom. "And I didn't want any brown babies in this family."

The world spun. A reporter's pen hit the floor with a clatter like gunfire. Two jurors recoiled. Someone in the gallery sobbed. Derrick made a sound like trying to breathe through glass.

"I loved her," he choked, bowing over his hands. "I loved her."

Nicole stood before she knew she'd moved. Her voice came out level only because rage and sorrow propped it up on either side. "Your honor, the State moves to dismiss all charges against Derrick Reddick and asks that Mrs. Evelyn Reddick be taken into custody for the murder of Bianca Laurent."

Judge Price's gavel cracked like lightning. "So ordered." He turned to the bailiffs. "Take the witness into custody."

Evelyn tried to rise with dignity and found none. The cuffs clicked, cold punctuation.

"I did it for you," she cried as they led her away. "For your future!"

Derrick couldn't look at her. No one could.

Judge Price gazed at the jurors. "I want to thank you for your service. You are now dismissed."

He rose and exited the chamber.

Court dissolved into human noise, jurors shepherded away, the gallery emptying in a messy current of shock, cameras lowered, whispers rising like steam. The official words, *adjourned, dismissed,* bounced off wood and marble and meant, for once, something like mercy.

Nicole sat because her knees decided they were done pretending. She was prosecutor enough to be grateful, woman enough to hurt. Justice was never clean. It cut on both sides.

The truth slid cold through her veins: twenty years ago, she could have been in Bianca's place, different faces, same history, same trap.

She waited until the room had thinned, then gathered her files with careful hands and walked out on legs that felt like somebody else's. The hallway was cool. The fluorescent lights hummed. She pushed through the first door on the left, the ladies' room, and locked herself into a stall before the tremble reached her fingers.

For a long minute, all she could do was breathe. In. Hold. Out. Count the tiles. Count her heartbeats. Tell herself she was fine, even as her body told the truth.

When she finally stepped to the sink, her reflection stared back: composed, yes, but cracked at the edges. She pressed cold water into her wrists, then to her eyes. The past unspooled behind her like a film.

Seventeen. A sundress. A Mustang waiting, full of summer and forever. A parlor that smelled like lemon oil and judgment. Tripp's mother, another elegant predator, explaining in a tone meant to pass for kindness that her son would never marry Nicole.

Nicole had stood her ground that day, shaking so hard,

she thought her bones might rattle, and said no. It hadn't mattered. The outcome had been the same: a future closed like a door in her face. A boy she'd loved going silent. Two families, deciding their fate.

And now Bianca.

Nicole pressed her palms to the counter until her ring bit skin. "I'm sorry," she whispered, not sure to whom, Bianca, the unborn child, the seventeen-year-old version of herself who hadn't known how to survive the avalanche. "I'm so, so sorry."

The door opened. The woman who slipped in had streaks of gray braided into her hair and the kind of eyes that had cried more than once. Bianca's mother. She met Nicole's gaze in the mirror. Something like gratitude quivered there. Something like ruin.

"You fought for her," the woman said softly. "Thank you."

Nicole's throat worked. "He did too." She paused. "We should have all fought sooner, before it became a murder."

The woman nodded once, as if they had exchanged something sacred and enough, and left.

Nicole dried her hands, squared her shoulders, and reassembled herself. Work first. Breakdown later.

In the corridor, the light found Tripp before she did. He stood by the stairwell door, jacket unbuttoned, tie loosened. For a heartbeat, he was eighteen again and everything was simple. Then the stairwell yawned behind him, and she remembered every complicated thing.

He didn't speak as she approached. He just watched her.

The look stripped away the room, the noise, the years. It scared her how much she wanted to step into it.

"You okay?" he asked at last.

"Define okay." She managed a ghost of a smile. "I've been better. I've been worse."

"I'm sorry, this case seemed to parallel our own lives." His voice was low, roughened by something she didn't want to name.

"Different people. Same song."

His jaw shifted. For a second, she thought he might say her name the way he used to, make it a place she could go. Instead, he said, "You did the right thing in there."

"So did you." She glanced down the corridor toward the emptying courtroom. "You saved him. You gave Bianca… you gave her mother the truth."

"We both did." He looked at her longer than was safe in a hallway with windows. "Nicole—" He broke off, rubbed the back of his neck. "When I called Evelyn, I thought I knew how it would go. I didn't know…" He swallowed. "I didn't know it would sound like that. I suspected her of murder."

"Neither did I." Her voice frayed. She pulled it taut again. "But now we do."

A silence opened, filled with everything they hadn't said for years: I tried. I failed you. I was scared. They made me choose. I let them. I'm still angry. I'm still here.

He stepped aside, opening the stairwell door like a gentleman in a bygone century. She slipped into the cool echo of concrete and metal, and he followed.

"Tonight," he said softly. "Seven. The restaurant on Sixth, the corner booth they always try to save for the judge." The corner of his mouth lifted. "I bribed the hostess. She still owes me three favors."

Nicole stared out the window at the reporters. A shiver rippled through her. If she said yes, she wasn't just agreeing to dinner. She was agreeing to open the door that the past had slammed shut to see what had survived on the other side.

"Say no if you need to," he added, so gently she could have cried. "Say later. Say never. I'll take what you give."

She looked up. The blue of his eyes was older now, complicated, capable of both mercy and cross-examination. The man who had cut a mother to the bone in defense of a son also looked like someone who could learn to hold a woman's heart carefully this time.

"I'll be there," she said, and the ache that had lived under her sternum for years shifted, made room.

His breath left him, almost a laugh. "Seven," he repeated, softer.

She nodded and turned to go before she changed her mind.

Outside, the sky was a hot, relentless blue. Reporters waited at the bottom of the steps, microphones like the heads of curious birds. Derrick stood a few yards away, shoulders hunched, his lawyer at his side. When he saw Nicole, he straightened, eyes red-rimmed but steady. For a moment, they simply looked at each other, prosecutor and almost-victim, the shape of a life returned to him still unfamiliar.

"I'm sorry," she said quietly when she reached him. "For what you lost. For what I couldn't see soon enough."

He nodded. "Thank you," he managed. "For…not making it about winning."

"It was never about that." And today, at least, that had been true.

She left him to the cameras and the questions, to the sweep of a life that had changed too quickly. She walked down the steps into the noise, into the heat, into the city that would not pause for grief. A breeze teased the hem of her skirt and, on its back, for the first time in years, came the fragile scent of something like hope.

Tonight at seven, she would sit in a corner booth and decide if the past had to own the future. She would tell the seventeen-year-old version of herself, shaking, furious, unbroken, that sometimes justice arrived late but still arrived. That sometimes the truth didn't heal you cleanly, but it could set the bone right so it could knit.

Nicole lifted her face to the sun, closed her eyes, and let the light find every cracked place. Then she opened them again and kept walking.

CHAPTER 20

The restaurant was one of those quiet coastal places that looked out over the water, all soft lighting and dark wood, the kind of place couples lingered in corners with wineglasses between them. Nicole sat at a table near the window, her untouched glass of chardonnay catching the glow of the candles.

She checked the time again. Six fifty-nine.

Her pulse thudded like a gavel in her chest. She had tried to tell herself this was just a conversation, two attorneys, two former friends, nothing more. But the lie wouldn't stick. Not when her stomach felt knotted and her throat too tight, not when she still carried the echo of his voice and the storm in his eyes after court.

Then he walked in.

Tripp's broad shoulders filled the doorway as though the whole room had been waiting for him. His suit jacket was gone, his tie loosened, but he still looked like command in motion. His gaze swept the room until it found her, and something inside her trembled.

Something inside her broke loose and traveled all the way to her center.

He came to the table, and for a beat, neither of them spoke. Then he managed a small, almost rueful smile. "Seven o'clock sharp. You always did like punctuality."

Nicole's mouth curved despite herself. "And you always cut it close."

He slid into the seat across from her. For a long moment, they simply looked at each other, the silence not hostile but weighted with too much history.

Every spark remained, the attraction, the passion, the longing, all of it alive, just as powerful as the first time they'd fallen for each other as teenagers.

Finally, Nicole said softly, "Today was hard."

Tripp nodded, his throat working. "For both of us." He let out a long breath. "I keep thinking about Evelyn. About what the jury saw. About how easily it could have been... hidden forever."

Nicole's fingers tightened around her wineglass. "That's what terrifies me. Twenty years ago, it could've been me. The circumstances were different, but the power behind them was the same. Parents pulling strings. Deciding who we should and shouldn't be with. Ending a love."

His eyes locked on hers, raw and unguarded. "I thought I was protecting you then. But I see now, I wasn't protecting either of us. I let them win. I should have torn the world apart to get to you, but I was too broken, too convinced you'd shut me out. I believed that damn email, and it poisoned everything."

Her throat ached. She blinked hard, but the tears burned anyway. "And I let them too. I didn't fight hard enough. I should have gone with you that morning. I should've trusted us more than I trusted them."

A muscle jumped in his jaw. He reached across the table, covering her hand with his. His palm was warm, steady, and the touch made her breath catch.

"No," he said hoarsely. "Don't take that on yourself. We were kids. They were the ones who schemed, who lied, who decided they knew better. We were just… caught."

Her first tear slipped free. She didn't swipe it away.

Tripp's thumb brushed the back of her hand, slow and tender. "I don't want to live in the half-light anymore, Nic. Not with you. If we're ever going to move forward, we need to know exactly what they did. Both of them. All of them."

She swallowed, her voice trembling. "You're saying… bring them together. Make them talk."

Forcing them all into the same room would be a gamble, a dangerous one, but it might be the only way. The risk of explosion hung heavy, but so did the promise of release. No more lies. No more intrigue. Just a reckoning waiting to happen.

"Yes." His gaze was fierce, determined. "Put every lie on the table. Drag it into the light. And then, whatever comes after, it's ours to decide. Not theirs."

Her thoughts turned to her mother—so proud, so

polished. But would she be honest when it mattered? Her father was straightforward, almost to a fault, but her mother...her mother had always preferred secrets, hoarding them like weapons, pulling them out only when they cut the deepest.

Her heart twisted. It was terrifying. It was necessary.

"Yes," she whispered. "We do it together."

The words felt like a vow.

Tripp's expression softened. Relief mingled with something deeper, something that had never really died between them. His thumb traced her hand again, lingering. "God, I've missed you."

Nicole let out a shaky laugh through her tears. "You've seen me every day in court."

"Not like this," he said. His voice was low, rough. "Not where I can touch you."

The world narrowed until it was just him, his hand over hers, his eyes burning into her. The years fell away, the prom nights, the stolen kisses, the wild hope of running away together. Her body remembered all of it, and the longing that had slept for too long roared awake.

She rose first, unable to sit still against the pull between them. Tripp followed, dropping bills on the table without even glancing. Neither of them spoke as they walked through the restaurant, through the curious stares, into the cool night.

Outside, under the glow of a streetlamp, she turned to him. Her voice was almost a whisper. "Tripp..."

He didn't let her finish. His hands framed her face, and then his mouth was on hers.

The kiss was desperate, searing, years of grief and want colliding. She gasped against him, then melted into it, her hands clutching at his shirt, pulling him closer. Tears streaked her cheeks, but she didn't care. Not when his lips claimed hers like he'd been starving for them.

They broke apart only to breathe, foreheads pressed together.

"Too many years," he murmured.

"Too many," she whispered back.

And then they were kissing again, deeper, hungrier, oblivious to the world around them.

When he finally pulled back, his breath ragged, his eyes dark with heat, he said, "Not here. Not like this. Come with me."

Her heart thundered. She didn't ask where. She just nodded.

She'd dreamed of this night for years, imagined it a hundred different ways, the moment they found their way back to each other, the first time she melted into his arms again. Now, as it finally loomed real, a shiver of unease spiraled through her. And yet nothing—no fear, no doubt, no ghost of the past, could keep her from him tonight. Nothing.

Minutes later, his car pulled into the gravel lot of a nice seaside hotel, the kind with balconies that faced the ocean. It should have felt tawdry, reckless. Instead, it felt inevitable, the only place their twenty years of longing could finally break free.

The elevator crawled upward, every second stretching like an eternity. When his hand closed around hers, her breath hitched, anticipation coiling tightly inside her. God, what was wrong with this elevator? Why did it feel like it was moving through molasses when all she wanted was for the doors to open?

Inside the room, the door barely clicked shut before his mouth was on hers again. Kisses rough, tender, urgent, all at once. Her fingers fumbled with his tie, his hands skimming her back, pulling her closer, needing her as much as she needed him.

This time, she didn't stop herself.

This time, there would be no running away.

CHAPTER 21

Tripp had managed a room at the nicest hotel on the gulf facing the ocean. He didn't care about the cost. He only wanted to give Nicole the best. This was not the night they stayed in a cheap motel when they were kids.

This was a new beginning. The hotel room door shut with a soft click, sealing them into quiet. The hum of the air conditioner filled the silence, faintly mixed with the smell of salt drifting through the old balcony door. The place was glamorous, the best he could get on such short notice.

Yet standing here with Nicole, it felt like the most intimate place he'd ever been.

She leaned against the door, her hand pressed flat against it as if to steady herself. The light from the bedside lamp spilled across her skin, catching in the strands of her ebony hair, making her look like a portrait he'd dreamed and lost and somehow found again.

For a moment, he couldn't move. He was afraid this was a dream, that if he blinked too long, she'd vanish.

"I don't want to waste another second," he said, his voice low and rough.

Her lips parted, trembling. "Then don't."

That was all it took. He crossed the space and caught her face in his hands, kissing her like a starving man who had just been given bread. The touch of her mouth sent fire through him. She tasted of wine and salt, but underneath was something that was only Nicole, familiar, intoxicating, and devastating.

She melted into him, her arms twining around his neck, pulling him closer, as if she, too, had been waiting years for this moment. Her body pressed tightly to his, soft against hard, and the sound she made, a quiet gasp that broke into a sigh, nearly unraveled him.

"God, I've missed you," he whispered against her mouth, pressing frantic kisses to her jaw, her temple, the hollow of her throat.

Tonight, the moment her hand slipped into his, it felt like coming home, as if every road he'd taken had been leading him right back here. This was where he belonged, where he'd always belonged. And he swore, then and there, nothing, no one, was ever going to rip this away from him again.

"Too many years," she breathed, her hands clutching his shirt, tugging, desperate.

"Never again." His vow was harsh, almost broken, against her skin. He kissed the line of her throat, felt her pulse leap beneath his lips, and nearly lost himself.

His hands slid down her arms, over her waist, reacquainting themselves with the curves that had haunted his memory. She trembled, not with fear but with want. When his fingers found the zipper at the back of her dress, she caught his wrist, her breath ragged. For a heartbeat, he froze, but then she lifted her gaze to his. Her eyes glistened with tears, but her voice was steady.

"Are we really doing this?"

He cupped her face with his free hand, his thumb brushing away a tear that spilled down her cheek. "We've been doing this since we were married. We just let everyone else get in the way. Not anymore."

Her breath hitched, and her grip loosened. "Then don't stop."

The zipper slid down, a whisper against the quiet. Fabric gave way and slid from her shoulders, pooling at her feet. The sight stole his breath. Lace clung to her body, delicate and devastating.

"Beautiful," he said, reverent.

She flushed, but her chin lifted, bold in her vulnerability. She reached for his shirt, her hands unsteady as she fought with the buttons. He covered her fingers, stilling them for a moment just to feel her touch. "Slow," he said, though the pounding of his heart urged anything but. "I want to remember every second."

Her answering smile was watery and fierce. "Then remember this."

Her palms slid beneath his shirt, over his chest, tracing muscle and scar, leaving heat in their wake. When her fingers brushed the hollow just above his heart, he felt undone, as if she'd reached past bone and flesh to the core of him.

Why had it taken them this long to find their way back to each other? So many years wasted, so many moments stolen-time they could never get back.

Twenty years gone, and love had been the casualty.

Clothes fell away in a blur. The carpet was littered with fabric, but neither cared. They stumbled back toward the bed, mouths fused, laughter breaking out once when he tripped on his slacks, then dissolving again into a kiss that burned away everything but need.

When her bare skin pressed against his, her heat seared him. He felt her ribs rise and fall against his chest, her hands splaying along his back, her legs tangling with his as she pulled him closer. Every nerve lit up. He kissed her harder, slower, softer, desperate to taste every part of her he had been denied for so long.

They found the mattress, and he lowered her onto it with a care that belied the urgency in him. Hovering above her, he braced his weight, staring down at her. The lamplight painted her in gold and shadow, the softness of her mouth, the sheen of tears that hadn't yet fallen.

"Tell me this is real," he rasped, his voice hoarse.

Her hands framed his face, her thumbs brushing his jaw. "It's real. It's always been real."

Something broke inside him then. He kissed her again, tasting tears and salt and fire, and when she opened to him, when her body arched into his, he moved with her. Slow, deep, savoring, until she gasped his name and clung to him as though she would never let go.

Every movement was a reclamation. *This is ours. This was always ours.*

The rhythm grew, steady, then urgent, their bodies remembering each other in ways their minds had tried to forget. Her nails raked gently down his back, her breath stuttered in his ear, her thighs locked around him.

"Tripp," she whispered, voice breaking. "I never stopped."

Emotion surged so strongly, his chest ached. "I know," he groaned, kissing her hard, as if he could pour every regret and every promise into her mouth.

The pace quickened, wild, until she cried out beneath him, her face alight with release, and he followed her, shattering with a force that left him trembling.

He collapsed against her, their hearts pounding in unison, sweat dampening their skin. He pressed his lips to her temple.

"I love you," he whispered, the words raw and unguarded.

She turned her head, meeting his gaze. Tears streaked her cheeks, but her smile was luminous. "I love you too."

He kissed her again, slow and tender this time, as if sealing a vow.

It was as if they'd stepped straight out of their wedding night and into this moment, the years between them erased. Nothing had truly changed—the love still surged between them, steady and unstoppable, flowing like a river that had never run dry.

All those years lost, and still, she was his.

The night stretched into something timeless. They moved together again, slower now, discovering and rediscovering. Between kisses, they whispered truths they'd been too afraid to say for years. She told him she had compared every man to him and found them all wanting. He admitted he'd buried himself in work because nothing else could numb the loss. Each confession was a thread pulling them closer, binding them together.

When exhaustion finally claimed them, they fell asleep tangled in hotel sheets, his arm locked around her waist, her breath warm against his chest.

Morning sunlight streamed through the thin curtains, golden and soft. Tripp stirred, the hum of the ocean outside the balcony filtering into his half-dreams. He blinked awake to find Nicole curled against him, her hair spilling across the pillow, her leg draped over his.

For a moment, he just lay there, memorizing her in the morning light. This wasn't a dream. She was here.

Carefully, he slipped free, pressed a kiss to her temple, and crossed to the corner of the room. The coffeemaker sputtered to life, filling the air with the sharp scent of brewing coffee. He poured two mugs, the steam curling upward.

Sliding open the balcony door, he stepped outside. The ocean stretched endlessly, its surface glittering under the rising sun. He took a deep breath, letting the salty air fill him, a peace settling into his bones he hadn't felt in decades.

No matter what the future held, he wanted her at his side. He would fight for her, move heaven and earth if he had to, and never again let anything—or anyone—tear them apart. Not even his mother. Especially not his mother.

Behind him, the door opened softly. Nicole appeared, wrapped in the motel blanket, her hair tousled, her eyes still heavy with sleep.

Seeing her now pulled him straight back to that first morning they'd woken as husband and wife—the glow in her eyes, the way she'd stolen his breath. Only now, she was even more beautiful, time and heartache somehow shaping her into the woman he could never stop wanting.

She'd been his then, and God help him, she was even more his now.

He handed her a mug. Their fingers brushed, and she smiled, small and secret, like they were sharing the best-kept secret in the world.

"This feels amazing," she said, gazing out at the ocean and then looking at him.

"Like the first day of the rest of our life," he said.

A blush filled her cheeks, and she reached out and took his hand.

They stood side by side at the railing, sipping coffee, watching the tide pull in and out. The silence was companionable, deep, a balm to everything they had endured.

Finally, Nicole tilted her face toward him. "We still have to face them," she said quietly. "All of them. And learn the truth."

Tripp nodded, slipping his arm around her shoulders. "We will. Together. This time, it's ours to decide."

She leaned into him, her head against his shoulder. "Then whatever comes… we'll survive it."

All he wanted was to drop to one knee and ask her to be his forever, to finally finish what they'd started twenty years ago. But before they could claim the future waiting for them, they had to confront the past and burn away every lie that had ever stood between them. Only then would the future truly be theirs.

And when the past was finally buried, he would put a ring on her finger and never let her go again.

He kissed the top of her head, pulling her closer beneath the blanket.

For the first time in twenty years, he believed her.

CHAPTER 22

It had been over twenty years since Nicole had been in Tripp's family home, which felt cold and loveless.

Suzanne Masterson's living room was as pristine and suffocating as Nicole remembered. The white marble floors gleamed, the chandelier glittered, the faint perfume of roses clung to the air. Everything about the house screamed of control, power, perfection, and exclusion.

Nicole sat stiffly on the sofa. Her parents perched nearby, nervous and pale. They hadn't wanted to come today, but she'd insisted.

Suzanne entered with her usual regal grace, pearls gleaming at her throat, her presence commanding the space.

"Let's not waste time," Suzanne said coolly. "I have guests arriving later. We all know why we're here."

What had she ever done to that woman to deserve such

contempt, other than being born without money or power in her veins? She'd clawed her way up, graduated at the top of her class, earned her law degree, and built a reputation as one of the best prosecutors in the state. And still—it wasn't enough. Nothing would ever be enough for Suzanne Masterson.

Why was she not good enough to marry her son?

Nicole's pulse hammered. "Tell me. Tell us everything you've kept from us."

Tripp crossed the room and slid his hand into hers, the gesture firm, deliberate. It wasn't just comfort, it was a statement. They stood together now, side by side, no longer the kids their parents could bully or manipulate. Yet the air in the room bristled with tension, every glance sharp, every silence heavy. It didn't feel like family. It felt like stepping onto hostile ground.

With Tripp's hand in hers, she finally felt strong enough. This time, she wouldn't stand alone, and she wouldn't back down.

Suzanne's smile was small, sharp. "Very well. Twenty years ago, when you and my son ran off like children and married, you forced our hands. That marriage could not stand. You were far too young, too foolish, and certainly mismatched."

"We were in love," Nicole said, her voice shaking but fierce.

Did the woman even have a heart, or had she traded it long ago for diamonds and social standing? Cold, detached, obsessed with things that meant nothing, Suzanne Masterson's only true love had ever been wealth and status, and she worshiped them like gods.

And she'd sacrificed everyone else at their altar.

Suzanne's lip curled. "Love doesn't last. Reputation does. Future does. My husband, God rest his soul, saw it clearly. He drafted the annulment papers himself. Together, we arranged everything."

Tripp's jaw tightened. "What do you mean *arranged?*"

Nicole felt the tension rolling off Tripp, saw the anger tightening his jaw, and she squeezed his hand hard, a silent reminder of the promise they'd made—to stay calm, no matter what came out, no matter what truths they unearthed. But, God, she hadn't realized how excruciating it would be to sit there and listen to the way their marriage had been deliberately sabotaged.

Suzanne looked at Tripp as though she were explaining something to a child. "We created the emails. Your father created yours, and Maria created Nicole's. Both claiming you'd made a mistake. You each believed the other had walked away."

Nicole's stomach dropped. "No…"

She'd known her parents had a hand in it, but hearing the truth out loud and learning their part in this tragedy was a wound she hadn't been prepared for. It cut deeper than she thought possible.

Her own mother had crafted the email to Tripp.

Maria's sob broke the silence. "It's true."

Her father's voice was low and rough. "They offered us money. Seventy-five thousand dollars. Enough to put you through college and even fix up the house. We told ourselves it was for the best. That you'd thank us someday."

Nicole staggered to her feet, her throat burning. Tears filled her eyes. Tripp's parents had offered money to end their marriage. Blood money to buy her out of his life. How could they? The realization drove into her like a knife to the chest, sharp and merciless, the betrayal cutting so deep she could hardly breathe.

The people she'd trusted had more than just deceived her. "You sold me. You sold my marriage for a check."

Her father looked stricken. Her mother's hands shook around her handkerchief.

Suzanne's eyes glittered. "We did what had to be done. My husband handled the paperwork. We took Dustin to Europe until it was complete. By the time he returned, the annulment was final. Clean. Erased."

For that witch, it had been nothing more than a tidy cleanup on aisle five. But it wasn't spilled groceries she swept aside—it was Nicole and Tripp's life. Their love. Their future. She'd swept it all into the trash without a second thought.

She hadn't just meddled, she'd destroyed.

Did Tripp know what they'd done?

Nicole turned to Tripp, pain burning through her. "Did you know?"

His face was pale, fury trembling in his hands. "I knew nothing."

Her knees weakened. Twenty years of silence, of heartbreak, explained in a handful of words.

They hadn't failed each other, their parents had failed them.

Suzanne rose, her expression triumphant. "And now you've come crawling back to each other, thinking you can rewrite history. But nothing has changed. I will never accept you, Nicole. Not then. Not now. Not ever."

"Mother—" Tripp's voice broke. "Don't say something you'll regret."

Nicole caught the way Tripp's fist clenched at his side, anger radiating off him in waves as his mother's venom dripped her name. Suzanne Masterson didn't just disapprove—she wanted Nicole erased. Cast out. Not now, not ever. The words stung, sharp as glass, but Nicole lifted her chin. She'd been broken once by this woman's contempt. Never again.

"No," Suzanne snapped. "If you choose her, you go against me, against everything our family name stands for. She will always be beneath you, and I will never give her a place in this house."

The woman hated her.

Tears stung Nicole's eyes. Why would she ever want to tie herself to his family? No matter how deeply she loved Tripp, she would always be an outsider. Their children would be born unwanted, unloved, judged by the same cruel standards. How could she ever build happiness on a foundation that told her, again and again, she would never be enough?

She turned to Tripp, her heart splintering. "I can't do this right now. I need time. I need to breathe." Despite all that she'd said about not letting his mother get between them, she couldn't imagine Tripp being ripped away from everything that mattered to him. Even though he loved her now, would he come to regret giving up his family for her?

His grip on her hand tightened; she could see the fear in his eyes. "Don't let her win again. Please, Nicole."

Her voice cracked. "I'm sorry. I love you. But I can't. I need some time."

She pulled her hand free and turned to her parents. "We're leaving."

They rose quickly, her mother dabbing at her eyes, her father silent, grim. Nicole didn't look back at Tripp because if she did, she wouldn't be able to walk away.

The car ride was suffocating. Nicole drove, tears streaming unchecked down her face. Her father couldn't drive any longer, and her mother, she feared, would not have found her way to the Masterson's home. But now she just wanted to get away from them.

"How could you?" she whispered at last, her voice raw. "How could you take their money? How could you let them erase my marriage? My life?"

CHAPTER 23

The door shut behind Nicole with a hollow thud that seemed to echo through his chest. He stood rooted in his mother's immaculate living room, staring at the space where she'd been only moments ago, his hand still tingling from where she'd pulled free.

She was gone.

Gone because of Suzanne. Because of the truth that had finally clawed its way into the light. And it was so damn ugly.

Slowly, Tripp turned. His mother was smoothing her blouse, her diamond earrings catching the lamplight, her expression composed, though the faint gleam in her eyes betrayed satisfaction.

"Well," she said, her voice cool as ice. "I suppose that settles it. She finally saw sense. Marianne is coming for dinner tonight."

Rage surged up his spine. "Sense?" His voice was low,

shaking with the effort to contain it. "You call destroying our marriage, fabricating lies, paying her parents to lie to her, sense?"

Suzanne's gaze was steady, her chin lifting. "I call it necessity. You were children. You would have ruined each other. Now, go get changed. Marianne should be here within the next hour."

"We loved each other," Tripp ground out. "We were married. Do you understand that? Married. And you erased it."

"Corrected it," Suzanne said crisply. "The annulment was the only solution. And I'd do it again."

His hands curled into fists. For years, he'd swallowed this woman's toxin, convinced himself she only wanted what was best. But tonight, watching Nicole's face shatter under the weight of Suzanne's cruelty, something in him had snapped for good.

"You disgust me," he said, his voice raw.

Suzanne blinked, momentarily startled. "Excuse me?"

"You heard me." He stepped closer, his height towering over her. "I'm done. You've interfered in my life for the last time. You stole twenty years from me, and tonight you drove away the only woman I've ever loved. I won't give you another chance to destroy what's left."

Her composure wavered, just slightly. "You're over-wrought. Sit down. We'll discuss this rationally in the morning. But tonight, Marianne will be here to have dinner with you. I arranged it all."

She never gave up. Not even after he'd told her he did not want to have anything to do with the woman.

"No," Tripp snapped. "There is no morning. Not with you. Not anymore."

Her mouth opened, but he cut her off, his words spilling hot and unrelenting. "You've controlled everything, my choices, my relationships, my future. Even now, you think you can dictate who I love, who I build my life with. But I'm finished being your pawn. If you want to keep living in this mausoleum of control, do it alone. Because I'm walking out that door, and I won't be back."

Her eyes narrowed, sharp with disbelief. "Don't be dramatic, Dustin. You have responsibilities. The practice—"

"The practice?" His laugh was bitter. "If you want to sell it, do it. If you want to burn it to the ground, burn it. It's yours. I'm not tethered to it anymore. Or to you."

"You can't mean that," Suzanne said, her voice faltering for the first time.

"I mean every damn word."

He turned, striding toward the hallway. His mother followed, her heels clicking on the marble. "Where are you going?"

"To pack my things."

"Don't be ridiculous—"

He spun, fury snapping through him. "Ridiculous? You fabricated emails. You bribed her parents. You shipped me off like luggage and erased a marriage you had no right to touch. That was monstrous. I should have walked away from you twenty years ago. I won't make the mistake of staying now."

Her face paled, but her spine stiffened. "You're my son. You can't just walk out on me."

Tripp met her eyes, his own blazing. "Watch me. I'll be in a hotel until Saturday. I'm not staying here a moment longer."

He yanked open drawers, pulling out clothes and shoving them into a duffel. The sound of fabric hitting fabric filled the silence. He didn't bother folding. He didn't care.

Behind him, Suzanne lingered in the doorway, her mask beginning to crack. "Dustin, stop this nonsense. You'll regret it in the morning."

He yanked the zipper closed and turned, chest heaving, every word rough with years of pent-up fury. "The only thing I regret is letting you control me for this long. I should never have come back. I should have walked out the other night and never looked back. This time, I won't."

Her lips parted, her voice sharp but edged with something unfamiliar, fear. "You'd choose her over me?"

"Yes." The word was immediate, absolute. His gaze burned into hers. "Every time. A thousand times. She is everything you'll never understand, love, loyalty, truth. You'll never accept her, and that's fine. Because I don't accept you anymore."

"I'm your mother," she whispered, startled, almost pleading.

"No." His voice cracked, but it carried like a verdict. "You're a monster."

Tears pricked his eyes, hot and unwanted. He slung the duffel over his shoulder, his voice breaking yet steady. "Good-bye."

Suzanne's composure faltered. Her hand clutched the doorframe as though she needed it to stand. "Wait."

He froze, shoulders taut.

"You never met your grandparents, my family, and there's a reason for that." Her breath hitched. "They were… white trash."

Tripp blinked, stunned.

"I was once like Nicole," Suzanne confessed, shame and venom tangling in her voice. "And I would've done anything to claw my way out. Anything. I married your father for his money. And when I look at her, I see myself. I know what girls like that are capable of. Don't you see? I'm trying to protect you from becoming *him*."

The words sliced through him, clarity coming with them. It all clicked: the relentless attacks on Nicole, the endless contempt. It wasn't just cruelty. It was projection. His mother had spent her whole life punishing him for her own sins.

Now it all made sense, his parents' cold marriage, his father's quiet misery, his mother's relentless social climbing. She hadn't just wanted status, she needed it, fed on it like oxygen. She ruled their lives like a queen desperate to keep her crown, constantly comparing, competing, and clawing her way to the top of the society ladder. And in the process, she made everyone around her miserable.

Including Tripp.

But Nicole wasn't Suzanne. Nicole loved him. Fiercely. Honestly. Completely.

He searched her face, for once seeing the cracks, the hollowness behind the pearls and perfection. "Have you ever loved anyone? Truly loved them?"

Her lips trembled. Tears glossed her eyes. And then, quiet, shattering—"No."

"That's what I thought." His voice broke, but his resolve didn't. "I love Nicole. She's everything. And I won't walk away from her again. Good-bye, Mother."

He turned, heading for the stairs. She followed him, her footsteps frantic behind his.

At the door, her voice fell to a whisper, desperate and brittle. "You'll come back. You always do."

"Not this time."

And with that, he walked out into the night, the cool air hitting his face like freedom.

For the first time in years, Tripp felt the chains snap loose. His future was uncertain, Nicole was gone, devastated, and he had no idea how to win her back. But one thing was clear: he would never again let Suzanne Masterson decide his fate.

He was his own man now.

This time, he would fight for Nicole with everything he had. But, first, he had to prove to her, and to himself, that his mother no longer pulled the strings. He needed his own place, his own work, a life free of her shadow.

The little beachside bar glowed with strings of twinkle lights, casting the whole place in a warm golden haze. The surf rolled just beyond the open windows, its rhythm weaving through the laughter and clinking of glassware. The music was a blend of reggae and rock, playing softly in the background.

Two days had passed since the meeting with the parents, and Nicole hadn't felt this empty, this detached, since she left for college without Tripp. It was that same dull ache, like something had been carved out of her, and nothing had grown back.

Nicole almost stayed home, but even there, the air was uneasy, every silence sharp, as if they were all tiptoeing barefoot across seashells. Nothing felt safe anymore. It was time to slip away, to find a place where she could finally breathe.

She spotted her friends instantly: Paige, Crystal,

Jennifer, and Amanda gathered at a high-top near the window, their faces lit with easy camaraderie.

God, how she had missed these women—her lifeline, her laughter, her family of choice. She loved them fiercely, and tonight, all she wanted was to sink into their warmth, to forget the years of distance and heartache and simply enjoy their company. But the shadow lingered. She knew the questions would come, and they would want to know what had happened between her and Tripp. And that day… that wound…she wasn't sure she could rip it open again. Not yet.

For the first time since the disastrous meeting at Suzanne Masterson's house, Nicole felt herself exhale. These women would make her feel better. They would help heal her from the pain and maybe even help her decide what to do about Tripp, because right now, she wasn't certain.

Once again, her life felt like it had been tossed in the air, pieces scattering in every direction, her family, her career, and worst of all, her love life. She and Tripp had been so close to finding their way back to each other, only for the past to rear its ugly head and breathe fire over everything they'd fought to overcome. The dragon of betrayal had scorched the earth beneath their feet, and it had scorched them too.

And all she could see now were the ashes of what they might have been.

"Nicole!" Paige called, waving her over with a grin. She

lifted her glass of *water*, as if it were champagne, ice cubes rattling against the rim.

Nicole slid into the empty chair with a weary smile. "Sorry, I'm late. Work ran long."

Crystal, round and radiant in a soft maternity dress, raised her brows. "Nice try. You live ten minutes away. You just didn't want to come sit with four nosy women and answer a hundred questions."

That earned a ripple of laughter. Nicole laughed too, a little weakly, but she felt some of the heaviness in her chest ease.

And yes, she could already feel them circling, priming her for the details they were dying to hear.

The waiter swung by and took her order, a margarita, heavy on the lime. Paige tapped her water glass when he looked at her. "I'm pacing myself tonight," she said. "Someone's gotta keep the rest of you from dancing on the tables."

Jennifer leaned over. "That's a shame, Paige. You're usually the first one *on* the table."

"I've retired," Paige deadpanned. "Graceful exits only."

Amanda snorted into her mojito. "Until karaoke starts."

The women laughed again, and Nicole found herself almost smiling for real.

"To surviving another week," Amanda said, raising her glass. "Have I told you that dating at this age sucks?"

They all laughed.

"To surviving the trial," Jennifer added. "And not strangling opposing counsel, even though he's entirely strangle-able."

"Here, here," Crystal said, clinking her glass of ginger ale against Jennifer's.

Nicole lifted her margarita. "To friends who refuse to let me sulk in peace."

Glasses clinked, laughter rippled again, and for a moment Nicole let herself just be.

But her friends didn't let her off that easily.

Paige leaned in, her chin resting on one hand. "All right, spill. How's it really? Because every time I see you on the news, you look like a stone statue. Meanwhile, we know you're probably dying inside."

Nicole hesitated, then sighed. "It's over. Evelyn Reddick admitted to murdering Bianca."

"What?" Amanda said. "She's in the same social stratosphere as Suzanne Masterson. I guess the ultra-rich can commit murder and not get away with it."

Nicole nodded. "Tripp figured it out. Evelyn put Bianca's address into her GPS the night of the murder. She arrived ten minutes before the coroner said she died. He showed evidence of her leaving her house and the time she returned the night of the murder. He was excellent. And she planted the murder weapon in her son's apartment."

"And how do you feel about Tripp as a lawyer?" Paige asked.

Her voice cracked at the edges. "He's maddening. He's brilliant."

Crystal reached across the table, her fingers brushing Nicole's hand. "You still love him."

Nicole's throat closed. She couldn't say the words. But she didn't deny it either.

Of course, she still loved him. How could she not? She'd loved him for half her life. But every time they found their way back to each other, it seemed their families rose up like walls, standing between them and the love that refused to die.

They weren't each other's enemy, their families were.

Jennifer smirked into her straw. "Honestly, I don't blame you. The man looks like he stepped straight out of GQ. And when he stares at you in court, the rest of us need sunglasses."

Nicole laughed softly, grateful for the joke, though her chest still ached.

Paige twirled her straw through the ice in her water. "So… speaking of Tripp."

Nicole stiffened. "Paige…"

She couldn't talk about him tonight or she might break down crying.

"What?" Paige's smile was just a little too innocent. "I'm just saying maybe you don't know everything."

"You don't either," she said, thinking about what had happened after the trial ended.

"Tell us," Jennifer said. "We want all the juicy details."

For the next five minutes, she told them about how they had agreed to meet after the trial and discuss their marriage. They ended up spending the night at a hotel, and the next morning, they decided to bring their parents together and learn the truth of what happened twenty years ago.

When she got to the part about how Suzanne had treated her, a tear trickled down her cheek.

"Damn, that woman is a bitch," Amanda said.

"I'm so sorry, honey," Crystal said. "You don't deserve that."

"What did Tripp do?" Jennifer said, her voice angry. "Was he a man and did he stand up to his mother?"

That had been her biggest disappointment. Maybe he had after she left, but before she walked out, he'd just sat there staring at her in disbelief.

"I didn't give him the chance. I told my parents we were leaving. I told him I need time. It feels like all that we've gone through is still keeping us apart."

How could she tell them she'd felt so disappointed with how Tripp had responded, and how she feared Tripp would come to hate her for making him choose between his mother and her?

"Just a minute, Nicole. You don't know what happened after you left," Paige said, grinning.

Nicole narrowed her eyes. "What are you talking about?"

Paige sat back, folding her arms. "Don't shoot the messenger. But you should know, he's not living with his mother anymore."

Nicole froze. "What?"

Had the revelation sent him running? The thought

twisted in her gut. She'd been disappointed, crushed, but maybe he'd been reeling, too, as stunned as she was. She had never imagined their parents would stoop so low, go to such lengths just to rip them apart.

Who does that to their own children?

"He moved out," Paige said, her eyes gleaming with satisfaction. "Packed his bags, walked out of that mausoleum she calls a house. Suzanne's in full meltdown mode. I hear she's been calling everyone from the garden club to the church rector, trying to get Tripp to answer her. He won't."

Crystal's mouth dropped open. "You're kidding."

Paige shook her head. "Not a bit. And that's not all. This morning, he resigned from the firm. Just walked away. Suzanne's practically climbing the drapes because she can't control him anymore."

Nicole's heart thundered, her margarita forgotten. "He… he left?"

Stunned, she sat frozen, her mind spiraling. Where had he gone? And why, after everything, hadn't he reached out to her?

Paige's grin softened. "He left, Nic. He's done. With her. With everything she used to dangle over him."

Nicole shook her head, dazed. "But why would he—"

"Because of you," Jennifer cut in, sipping her drink with a flourish. "The man does have a set of balls, after all."

Nicole laughed bitterly.

Paige smiled. "No. Because he couldn't stand her controlling him anymore."

Amanda leaned forward, her eyes kind but firm. "Or maybe because he finally realized the only way to prove he deserves you is to cut her out of his life. You gave him the choice, Nicole. And he's choosing you."

Nicole's throat tightened. Tears pricked her eyes, but she blinked them back.

Crystal rubbed her belly thoughtfully. "I'll tell you what I see. I see a man who's finally fighting for you. He lost you once, and he's tearing down every wall to make sure it doesn't happen again. I'm surprised you haven't heard from him."

So was Nicole. The silence gnawed at her. Was he trying to prove, once and for all, that he was done letting his mother pull the strings? Or was he off somewhere preparing a place for them, trying to build a future she could finally believe in? Whatever the reason, the not knowing clawed at her. God, she just wished he would call, let her in, let her know what he was thinking.

The silence was starting to feel like abandonment all over again.

Nicole covered her face with her hands, her shoulders trembling. "I don't know if I can trust it. She said she'd never accept me. That our children would never be loved." Her voice cracked. "What if she's right? What if no matter what he does, I'll never be enough in that family's eyes?"

Her friends went quiet for a moment.

Then Paige set down her water with a sharp clink. "Nicole Reyes, listen to me. You're more than enough. Always have been. Suzanne Masterson is a miserable woman who only feels powerful when she makes others feel small. You're not small. You're brilliant. You're stubborn. You're the girl who made the golden boy of the island fall head over heels, and guess what? He still is. If he's cutting her out, then for God's sake, let him."

Amanda raised her mojito. "Hear, hear."

Jennifer leaned forward, her smile wicked. "Also, let's be honest: the man looks at you like you're oxygen. And unless I missed a memo, oxygen is non-negotiable."

Even Crystal laughed at that, her hand pressing to her belly as if to steady herself.

Nicole shook her head, tears slipping down her cheeks, but a small smile tugged at her mouth. "You all make it sound so simple."

"Love is simple," Crystal said gently. "It's the rest of the world that complicates it."

Nicole looked down at her glass. Paige's words replayed in her mind: *He moved out. He resigned. He's done with her.*

Her heart ached, but underneath the ache flickered something dangerous. Something she'd almost forgotten how to feel.

Hope.

Now, where was Tripp and why hadn't he called her?

CHAPTER 25

It was the annual Billfish Pachanga in Port Aransas and she'd let her friends talk her into attending. The community center buzzed with voices and laughter, the kind of small-island party where everyone seemed to know everyone. Strings of white lights looped across the ceiling, and music pulsed from a corner speaker. Nicole had almost stayed home, but Paige had insisted, and now here she was with her friends clustered around a table near the dance floor.

Crystal looked radiant in her flowing maternity dress, ginger ale in hand. Paige nursed her ever-present glass of water, scanning the crowd like a queen surveying her court. Amanda was already on her second mojito, teasing Jennifer about the guy in the navy blazer who couldn't stop staring at her.

Nicole tried to smile, tried to be present, but the weight of the last few weeks sat heavily in her chest. Even here, surrounded by her friends, she felt fragile, like a shell that would crack if anyone pressed too hard.

"Stop brooding," Paige said, nudging her. "You'll wrinkle."

Nicole rolled her eyes. "Thank you for your concern."

Jennifer leaned in, her dark eyes glinting. "She's not brooding. She's sulking."

"I'm not—" Nicole began, but Amanda cut her off with a laugh.

"Yes, you are. You've got that tragic heroine vibe going. Like you're waiting for Mr. Darcy to appear in the fog and declare undying love."

Crystal patted Nicole's arm. "Or maybe she's waiting for Tripp Masterson to walk in and ruin her night."

Nicole's stomach twisted. "He wouldn't come here."

Paige smirked. "Oh, wouldn't he?"

Before Nicole could ask what she meant, the crowd near the door shifted, and conversation dipped like a wave pulling back. She didn't have to look to know. Her pulse told her. Her skin told her.

Tripp.

He stood just inside the entrance, scanning the room. No tie, his shirt open at the collar, his jacket slung casually over his shoulder. He looked less like the polished attorney and more like the boy she'd once run away with, older, harder, but still the only man her heart had ever recognized.

"Speak of the devil," Jennifer murmured.

"Oh, he's no devil," Amanda said. "Not with that jawline."

Paige elbowed Nicole. "Well? Don't just sit there. Go talk to him."

Nicole's throat closed. "No."

But Tripp had already spotted her. His gaze locked, unshakable, and the rest of the room fell away. He started toward her, his stride steady, unstoppable, like he'd crossed the ocean to reach her.

Nicole's heart pounded so hard, she thought everyone must hear it.

It had been a week since their parents ripped the mask off and revealed the plan that had torn them apart. A week of sleepless nights, her mind gnawing on every fear that the past would never loosen its grip on them. And yet here he was, walking toward her—and every nerve in her body screamed yes.

God help her, she still wanted him more than air.

When he reached the table, her friends made a production of excusing themselves, Paige dragging Amanda toward the dance floor, Jennifer suddenly "remembering" she needed to refresh her drink, Crystal claiming she had to use the restroom, though Nicole knew she'd just been. In seconds, it was just the two of them.

"Nicole," he said, his voice low, the way he used to say it when no one else was around.

What was she supposed to do? His mother despised her with every breath, and yet Nicole loved this man more than life itself. A part of her was finished, finished trying to win over a woman who would never accept her. All she wanted was Tripp. To hell with family ties. But even as the thought hardened inside her, she couldn't ignore the truth, his mother still had the power to make their lives a living hell.

She looked up at him, forcing steel into her spine. "You shouldn't be here."

"I had to be."

The words hung between them, raw and unpolished.

"Tripp—" she began, but he held up a hand.

"Please. Let me talk before you send me away again."

She swallowed hard, her pulse racing. "Fine."

He pulled out the chair across from her and sat, leaning forward, elbows braced on his knees, his eyes never leaving hers.

"I'm done with her," he said. "With Suzanne. With everything she's used to keep me in her grip. I moved out. Packed my bags. I'm living in a hotel near the pier. I have a real estate agent looking for a property for me to buy."

Nicole's breath caught.

Paige had been right. He'd moved out and completely separated himself from his mother.

"I resigned from the firm," he went on, his voice steady, resolute. "She tried to talk me out of it, threatened, begged. I didn't care. I walked away. For the first time in my life, I am not living under her shadow. And I'm not going back."

He was proving, in the only way that mattered, that they were more important. Hope swelled in her chest, fierce and trembling. This, this was what she had longed for, what she had prayed for.

Maybe, finally, they had a real chance.

Nicole's chest ached, hope clawing its way into her heart, but fear sat heavier. "Why are you telling me this?"

"Because I need you to know," he said, his eyes blazing. "I need you to know I'm not the same boy who let her tear us apart. You don't know how much I regret not finding you and talking to you before I signed those papers. But I promise you, I will fight with everything I have. For you. For us."

"I have the same feelings. I wish I had spoken to you. But I was so young and so angry and hurt."

Tears burned her eyes. "Tripp—"

He shook his head, leaning closer. "No, listen. I'm not asking you to forgive overnight. I'm not asking you to forget twenty years of pain. But I am asking you to believe me when I say I choose you. I'll always choose you. I don't care if she never speaks to me again. I don't care if she disowns me, sells the house, or burns the firm to the ground. None of it matters if I don't have you. And I choose you."

Nicole's tears spilled, hot and unstoppable.

Tripp's voice broke then, softer but fierce. "We lost half our lives because of them. I don't want to lose another day. I want you, Nic. Just you. Marry me again. This time, no secrets. No parents. No interference. Just us."

Her breath hitched, her heart torn between terror and longing. "Tripp... I choose you. But Suzanne said she'll never accept me. That our children—" Her voice broke. "That our children would never be loved."

"Our children will be very loved by us. I can't wait for us to have babies." His jaw clenched. "We don't give her the chance. She'll never touch our children. She'll never touch you. Not again. I won't let her."

Nicole stared at him, her whole body trembling. She wanted to believe. God, she wanted to. And she knew that no matter what, she would always love him. It would always be Tripp.

Tripp reached across the table, took her hand, and pressed it to his chest. His heartbeat thundered beneath her palm. "Do you feel that? That's yours. It's always been yours."

The music swelled in the background, couples laughing and dancing, but Nicole heard only the thrum of his heart, the raw truth in his eyes.

For a long moment, she couldn't speak. Then, through the tears, her lips curved. "You're insane."

He smiled, a shaky, desperate smile. "So marry me."

Her laughter broke, half-sob, half-joy. "Tripp—"

"Not later," he said, standing, tugging her up with him. "Now. Tonight. Before anyone else tries to stop us. Let's elope."

Gasps rippled from a nearby table. Someone whistled. Nicole barely noticed. Her friends were suddenly there again, surrounding her, their faces beaming. Somehow, she got the feeling they knew about this little setup.

"Do it!" Paige whispered fiercely.

"Say yes!" Amanda squealed.

Crystal wiped at her eyes. "Go, Nicole."

Jennifer lifted her glass in salute. "About damn time."

Nicole looked at Tripp, at the boy she had loved, at the man who had finally broken free, and she knew this was the moment she'd been waiting for.

She nodded, tears spilling down her cheeks. "Yes. Yes, I'll marry you."

The room erupted in cheers, laughter, and applause, but Tripp pulled her into his arms, his mouth finding hers in a kiss that silenced everything else.

For the first time in twenty years, Nicole felt whole.

CHAPTER 26

The chapel looked smaller than she remembered. White clapboard walls glowed in the lantern light, the stained-glass windows reflecting a dozen flickering votives. The pews smelled of polish and old wood, the faint scent of lilies drifting from bouquets Paige had managed to charm out of the florist.

It was the same chapel where she and Tripp had stood twenty years ago, trembling with the thrill of first love, reckless enough to believe it was enough. The place where it had all begun, and where it had all been stolen.

Tonight, she was taking it back.

Her girlfriends were everywhere, orchestrating chaos. Paige stood at the front pew, water glass in hand like a queen's scepter. "Amanda, those ribbons are a disaster. Fix them. Jennifer, for the love of God, straighten that veil. And Crystal, stop waddling like a martyr. Sit down before you topple."

Crystal ignored her, belly-first, directing the placement of flowers with the authority of a general. "Left. More left. Yes, good. Perfect."

Amanda stuck her tongue out. "Bossy pregnant people are terrifying."

Nicole laughed softly, the sound shaky but real. "You're all insane."

"Insanely devoted," Paige said smugly. "Now quit fussing. You've got bigger things to worry about. Like marrying the man you never stopped loving."

Nicole's throat tightened. Her heart thumped so hard, she thought it might burst right out of her chest.

Tonight felt different, sacred, as if this was the night that would stitch everything back together. The past, the future, their very lives seemed to converge in this single moment. It felt better than their first wedding, richer, though touched with the strangeness of all they had endured to get here. And she loved every fragile, beautiful second of it.

It wasn't a beginning or an ending, it was coming home.

Then her parents entered quietly. Her father looked older, his shoulders stooped, but his eyes, when they met hers, were filled with something she hadn't seen in years: pride.

Her father stepped forward, voice rough. "Nicole… may I, may I walk you down the aisle this time?"

Tears pricked hot behind her eyes. She had dreamed of this moment, but never thought it would come. "Yes," she whispered. "Please."

It felt right, like the first fragile step toward forgiveness.

Her father's voice softened, carrying the weight of years they'd all lost. "You know, Tripp came to your mother and me and asked for your hand in marriage. And we told him we were thrilled. It's time to put the past behind us and heal, Nicole. Time for you and Tripp to create your future together. And I can't wait to see the grandchildren you'll give us."

The words cracked something open inside her. A sob slipped past her throat, raw and unguarded. He was right. It was time, time to stop bleeding from old wounds, to step into the future with Tripp, and finally leave the past where it belonged.

She wouldn't let the past steal one more day of their future.

Her father's grip was steady when she slid her hand into the crook of his arm. He leaned close, his words a confession. "I'm sorry, Nic. For the money. For the lies. For letting them tear you apart. We thought we were protecting you. We weren't. We were cowards."

Her tears spilled freely now. "I know, Daddy. And I forgive you."

Her mother's hand trembled as she pressed a handkerchief into Nicole's free hand. "You look beautiful, sweetheart. Don't mess up your makeup crying."

"I don't think I can keep from crying. This day has been so long in arriving."

Music began, Amanda's phone hooked to a tiny speaker, and the small crowd rose. Nicole took her first step down the aisle, her father beside her, and there was Tripp waiting at the altar.

He looked devastatingly handsome in his simple suit, his tie loose, his eyes locked on hers as though no one else existed. Her knees nearly gave beneath her, but her father held her steady.

Step by step, she walked toward the man she had loved since she was sixteen.

Her father squeezed her hand, then placed it in Tripp's.

"Take care of her," he said softly.

"I will," Tripp vowed, his voice breaking.

The officiant, a kind woman from the island who had been hastily called in, welcomed everyone, but Nicole hardly heard her. She could only hear the sound of Tripp's breathing, could only feel the warmth of his hand gripping hers.

The officiant smiled at the gathered friends and family, her voice rising clear against the hush. She gave a quick lecture on the sanctity of marriage and love before she asked the question that Nicole dreaded.

"If anyone here knows a reason why these two should not be joined in holy matrimony, speak now or forever hold your peace."

Nicole's breath caught. She knew this moment. Twenty years ago, no one had spoken, but later, voices had destroyed them anyway.

And then the doors creaked and slammed.

The entire congregation turned.

Suzanne Masterson walked in, pearls gleaming at her

throat, her face pale but proud. Nicole's blood ran cold. The silence was so deep that Nicole could hear her own pulse hammering.

Suzanne's eyes locked on her son. For a long, unbearable moment, she said nothing. Then, to everyone's shock, her voice cracked through the stillness.

"I object," she said, and the chapel gasped.

But she didn't stop there.

"I object to what I did twenty years ago. To the lies. To tearing you apart. To thinking I could buy and bully my way into controlling your happiness." Her voice faltered, her shoulders sagging. "I was wrong, Dustin. I thought I was saving you, but all I did was destroy the one thing that ever truly mattered. You once asked me if I had ever loved. The truth is, I did. You, my son, you were the one I loved. And I was wrong…so wrong…to destroy your trust."

Nicole's chest clenched. Tripp's grip on her hand tightened like a vow.

Suzanne's gaze shifted to Nicole then, softening in a way Nicole had never seen. "I was wrong about you too. You loved him when you were a girl, and you love him still. That kind of devotion isn't weakness. Its strength. And I was too proud to see it."

The chapel buzzed with whispers, but all Nicole saw was Tripp, his jaw hard, his eyes fierce as he turned to face his mother.

"This is Nicole," he said, his voice ringing with power. "My wife. My family. If you can accept her, you'll still have me. If you can't, then leave and don't come back. But hear me, Mother, this marriage stands. Tonight, tomorrow, always. No one will ever take her from me again."

The words struck like a gavel. The crowd seemed to lean in, breathless.

Suzanne's lips trembled. For a heartbeat, she looked like she might collapse under the weight of it. Then she gave a slight, shaky nod. Not triumph, not approval, but surrender.

"I won't stand in your way again. You have my blessing," she whispered. Then she sank slowly into a pew.

Nicole's chest heaved, her tears threatening anew. Tripp turned back to her, his eyes steady, fierce. *He had chosen. Publicly. Irrevocably.* The officiant cleared her throat softly. "Let us continue."

When it came time for vows, Tripp went first.

"I chose you then, Nicole Reyes," he said, his voice steady though his eyes shimmered. "I choose you now. And I'll keep choosing you every day we're given. No more secrets. No more shadows. Just us, together, as it always should have been."

Her tears fell freely, spilling down her cheeks. "You were my first love, Tripp Masterson. My only love. They tried to take it from us, but they never could. My heart remembered. My soul remembered. And I am yours. Forever."

The officiant nodded, smiling. "By the power vested in me… I now pronounce you husband and wife."

The chapel erupted in applause as Tripp pulled her into his arms and kissed her, a kiss that erased twenty years of pain. Her friends whooped, Crystal sobbed, Amanda yelled, "Finally!" and Jennifer snapped a picture with her phone.

A few minutes later, they burst through the doors, laughter tangled with tears, birdseed and flower petals raining down from their friends. And there, parked at the curb, sat a cherry-red Mustang convertible, gleaming under the lamplight.

Nicole gasped. "Tripp… it looks just like yours."

He grinned, tugging her toward it. "That's because I hunted one down. Thought we might need it tonight."

Her heart swelled until she thought it might split. They climbed in, her veil fluttering, his jacket tossed aside. When he revved the engine, the familiar growl sent a thrill down her spine.

Someone had tied Coke cans to the back and painted just married on the back window.

As they sped away from the chapel, from the shadows of the past and into the bright unknown, Nicole leaned close, laughter bubbling through her tears.

Twenty years ago, they'd run from the world. Tonight, they ran toward it.

Together.

CHAPTER 27

The bathroom door rattled as Crystal knocked for the third time.

"Paige? Are you done in there?"

That morning, Crystal had sent out an urgent call for all of them to meet at Paige's rental. Emergency gatherings were rare, almost unheard of, but today, every one of them had come.

From inside came a groan. "Would you quit rushing me? This is not like baking a pie. You can't just open the oven door every five seconds!"

Nicole, leaning against the hallway wall with Amanda and Jennifer, lifted her brows. "Should we be worried?"

Amanda smirked. "Depends. If she's in there with a bottle of tequila, yes."

Jennifer crossed her arms. "I told you. She's taking a pregnancy test."

Nicole's mouth fell open. "What? Who's the father?"

Crystal rolled her eyes at the group. "Yes, Sherlock. And, apparently, the apocalypse happens at the three-minute mark because she's been moaning about it the whole time."

Inside the bathroom, Paige snapped, "I can hear you, you know!"

Amanda grinned wickedly. "Good. We're judging you out here."

Nicole pressed a hand over her mouth to keep from laughing. The nerves in her stomach churned, not for herself but for her friend. She knew Paige well enough to know that control was her gospel, except when it came to men. There, she'd always flown by the seat of her stilettos, chasing freedom and living the single life to the fullest. But even Paige couldn't outmaneuver two little pink lines on a stick.

"Don't know," Crystal said. "I don't think it's anyone around here. Have you heard or seen her talking to anyone?"

"Just the pizza delivery boy, but he's way too young," Amanda said.

"Hey, I don't do youngsters," she replied from behind the door. "I like my men to know what they're doing."

They all laughed.

Finally, after what felt like forever, the door creaked open. Paige's face was pale, her eyes wide, and she held the plastic stick in her trembling hand. She looked at Crystal first, like she couldn't bring herself to face the others yet.

"Um," Paige said, her voice squeaky. "What does it mean when there's a pink plus sign?"

Crystal's grin spread slow and certain. "It means you're pregnant."

Paige's mouth fell open. "Oh crap."

Amanda whooped. "Called it!"

Jennifer's eyes widened. "Holy hell. Paige, are you serious?"

Nicole stepped forward gently, her heart squeezing at the sight of her usually unflappable friend looking so lost. "Oh, Paige…"

"I can't be pregnant!" Paige blurted, pacing the narrow hall. "I have a career. I have plans. I have… I have a yoga retreat booked in Tulum! Pregnant women don't sip cocktails in infinity pools!"

Amanda snorted. "Correction: pregnant women *shouldn't* sip cocktails in infinity pools. I've known some who tried."

"Not funny!" Paige snapped, though her voice wobbled. She pressed a hand to her forehead. "I don't even like children. They're sticky and loud, and they ruin throw pillows."

Crystal leaned against the doorframe, hands on her belly. "Yeah, I had doubts when one moved into my body and started practicing karate at two a.m. You get used to it."

Paige glared at her. "You are not helping."

Jennifer stepped closer, her tone calmer, steadier.

"Paige. Breathe. You're not in this alone. Whatever you decide, you have us."

Nicole nodded. "Always."

Paige looked around at their faces: Crystal, glowing and maternal; Amanda, smirking but soft-eyed; Jennifer, steady as bedrock; Nicole, glowing from her recent wedding. Her throat tightened.

"Why do you all look so happy?" she demanded. "This is not happy news. This is terrifying. I'd rather face a boardroom full of stuffy old white men than go through nine months of my body being inhabited by a tiny person."

Amanda grinned. "Because watching you lose your cool is the best entertainment I've had in weeks."

Nicole elbowed her. "Amanda!"

"What?" Amanda shrugged. "I'm being honest."

Crystal softened her voice. "Paige, listen. It's scary, yes. It changes everything. But it doesn't have to be bad. Sometimes the things we don't plan are the ones we end up being most grateful for." She rubbed her belly with a small smile. "Trust me. I didn't plan on a second one so quick."

Paige's lower lip trembled. She sank onto the hallway bench, clutching the test like it might bite her. "Pregnant," she whispered. Paige threw her hands in the air. "Pregnant. Me. Of all people. I've spent my whole life avoiding this exact scenario, careers, adventures, late nights, bad dates, you name it. And now, when I'm finally hitting my stride, two stupid pink lines show up and decide my entire future for me. God, I wasn't made for diapers and midnight feedings. I can't even keep a houseplant alive!"

Nicole crouched in front of her, laying a hand over hers. "You don't have to figure it all out tonight. But you also don't have to do it alone. We'll be here. Every step."

Paige's eyes shimmered with tears she refused to let fall. She huffed out a laugh, shaking her head. "God help this kid if Aunt Amanda is in charge of babysitting."

Amanda gasped in mock offense. "Excuse me, I am *excellent* with children. They love me. I teach them how to make faces at their parents. And I can't wait to teach yours."

She gave an almost evil laugh.

Jennifer sighed. "Exactly why you should *never* be in charge."

The laughter that broke out was shaky, but it loosened something in Paige's chest. For the first time since she saw the plus sign appear, she let herself smile, small, nervous, but real.

"No, I won't be marrying the father. He's already married. I won't even be telling him about the baby. And I guess this means I'm moving back to Mustang Island. Fort Collins would not be a good place for us to continue to reside if I want to keep this little secret."

"Yay," they all said together.

"We're so glad," Nicole replied.

"We can trade baby clothes," Crystal said.

"Don't look at me. My kids are grown," Jennifer replied.

"I can be your birthing coach," Amanda said with a grin. "We can start practicing your breathing exercises."

Paige shook her head in disbelief. "Dear God. I'm pregnant. How did this happen?"

"I think you had sex," Crystal said with a laugh. "I hope it was a good time."

With a sigh, Paige gazed at the women standing around her. "What am I going to do?"

"Have a baby," Nicole said.

Paige dropped her head into her hands. "Oh crap. There goes my carefree, single lifestyle."

"You're getting a little too old to be acting like you're still twenty," Jennifer said.

"It keeps me young," she said.

"Not anymore," Amanda said. "Welcome to motherhood."

Secrets of a Reckless Life Coming February 2026

THANK you for reading Nicole and Tripp's story. Mustang Island is quickly becoming some of my favorite stories. Next up will be Paige's story. Why do I think she's reckless? Because she has lived a wild life up until she learns she's pregnant. Oops!

He's grumpy, gorgeous, and deeply annoyed by her. It's perfect.

When Aisling O'Byrne catches her fiancé tangled in the sheets with her boss, she doesn't just leave—she *annihilates*. A few handcuffs, a Sharpie, and one very well-placed engagement ring later, Aisling walks out of her Manhattan life in flames… and into an inheritance she never expected.

Welcome to Mountshannon, Ireland: population nosy, scenic, and approximately 85% judging her. According to her late grandmother's will, Aisling must live in the crumbling O'Byrne mansion for six months to claim it. She plans to gut the place, sell it, and go back to pretending she has her life together. Easy.

Until she meets the infuriatingly broody—and unfairly

attractive—Ronan Gallagher, the man next door. He's her childhood betrothal turned adult nemesis, the local literary snob, and a man who seems to hate her *almost* as much as she hates his precious rose bushes.

As sparks fly and secrets surface—including a centuries-old family feud and the truth about her love-child past—Aisling begins to realize she might not be here to *escape* her story, but to *rewrite it*.

Available Everywhere!

I'LL BE HOME FOR CHRISTMAS

As Olivia Miller drove along the highway, the night hurled snow like Mother Nature spewed the white stuff.

The blizzard warnings were right. The wind howled, blowing her little hatchback all over the road while big flakes smacked the windshield like tiny snowballs. What was she doing out in this mess?

Music blared on the radio, and Olivia cringed at the Christmas carol that filled her car, asking for presents, snow, and mistletoe. Mother Nature was delivering on the snow.

"I'll be in Hell for Christmas," she sang changing the words, tears flowing down her cheeks as she thought about her miserable life.

This day couldn't get much worse.

The holiday season was supposed to be a beautiful,

happy time. A time of love and family, and damn it, this was going to be the worst Christmas ever.

Trying to watch the road, she wiped at the tears that had not stopped flowing since she'd left Billings. She'd waited until the last minute to leave, waiting around for the big jerk since he promised to go with her. And now she was on the road to Whitefish later than she planned. The storm they'd been predicting was upon her. In the dark, she watched as the snowflakes flew in the headlights, the wind shoving from lane to lane, her windshield wipers working overtime to remove snow.

Her sleigh was struggling and she wasn't feeling jolly, merry, or bright.

For the first time in years, her mother had issued a demand that the family gather at Christmastime for an important announcement and she'd thought that she and the jerk would be the center of that revelation.

In her mind, she'd dreamed of an engagement ring and a happily ever after with him asking her in front of her family. Only the dream was a nightmare, and she'd been the only one thinking of a pledge to marry. Not the big jerk.

The only disclosure she'd be making would be that she was still single and alone. That the man she'd thought was Mr. Right was actually Mr. All Wrong. Mr. All Wrong caught in bed with his coworker. Even now her eyes had a hard time unseeing the two of them entwined together, naked.

And then there was a second life-changing event that

had come completely out of the blue taking her by surprise.

The only thing that could be worse would be if she was pregnant. Thank goodness she'd been on the pill. Especially now.

Somewhere her life had taken a wrong turn and she'd found herself on a road she didn't know how to navigate. Until today, she'd thought that everything was going great. Then life imploded and everything that could go wrong, did, including the job she loved.

Fired.

So what was the family message if not her engagement? She'd not been home since she graduated from college. Time seemed to have gotten away from her and she'd been focused on the asshole and being the best at her career.

So much for the job and the man she loved.

This was not the first time she'd found a boyfriend cheating on her. What was wrong with her that she seemed to choose men who couldn't keep their dick in their pants?

With a sigh, she wondered how her sisters would react to the news that, once again, she was on her own. Once again, she'd caught her man in bed with someone else. She doubted her siblings ever had problems in regard to men. Especially Amelia, the golden girl.

One of the reasons she avoided going home was she knew she'd have to deal with her sisters. Why the urgency for the family to spend Christmas together? They'd grown up, and once they reached college, had become disconnected. By choice.

And now the twins would be there. The favored girls. No, not the oldest woman but two girls that could do no wrong. Amelia's life was always perfect. Head cheerleader, valedictorian, Mensa member, and scholarship winner.

Now a lawyer.

The family super achiever who probably had never broken a nail and her hair and makeup were always perfect and the world awaited her like a queen with her subjects. Bow down to Her Highness.

And Emma was a carbon copy, though she was the introverted twin. Still a super achiever, Emma kept her accomplishments more on the down-low compared to Amelia's shouting from the rooftops. A nurse in the NICU unit, she helped to save babies.

Olivia…she just plodded along, thinking everything was fine and then she discovered the truth. And nothing was right. None of her decisions, her career, everything gone to hell.

No one would ever call her an overachiever. And she doubted her sisters had ever been fired from their jobs.

The snow was beginning to pile up on the road and the few cars that had been on the highway suddenly disappeared. It was just her and a truck that had been behind her for the last several miles. When she reached the next town, she would find a hotel and spend the night.

Waiting for the big ass had been a huge mistake and now she was paying the price in more ways than one. Not only had he cheated on her, but he'd put her so far behind schedule to return home. The plan had been to leave at noon. At five, she gave up and went to his apartment. Mistake number two.

At this rate, she wouldn't make it home tonight. And maybe that was for the best. And yet she needed her mother's hug. It was the reason she'd not completely canceled.

Maybe the two of them could figure out where she'd gone wrong. And there was this supposed family announcement that her mother wanted everyone to hear.

In the white glare of her headlights, her brain realized an elk stood in the middle of the road like the king of the mountains. His size was intimidating and no match for her little car. The damn animal was staring her down, not moving. Her foot immediately moved to the brakes and when she hit them, her car began to spin on the snowy road.

Mistake number three. Don't slam on the brakes on ice and snow.

With a scream, she turned the wheel in the opposite direction and when she finally gained control, she saw the snow bank just as her car slammed into it.

Maybe this day could get worse. Her head smashed into the driver's door window and blackness came rushing toward her. Why had she waited on the big jerk? Why?

Available Everywhere

I'll Be Home
for Christmas
Come Home
for
Christmas
USA TODAY BESTSELLING AUTHOR
SYLVIA MCDANIEL

Contemporary Romance
Burnett Brides Contemporary Times
Travis
Tanner
Tucker
Joshua
Jacob
Justin
Cameron
Caleb
Cody
Desiree
Burnett Brides Contemporary Box Set Books 5-7
Burnett Brides Contemporary Box Set 8-10
Burnett Brides Contemporary Box Set 11-14

Return to Cupid, Texas
Cupid Stupid
Cupid Scores
Cupid's Dance
Cupid Help Me!
Cupid Cures
**Cupid's Heart
Cupid Santa
**Cupid Second Chance
Cupid Charmer
Cupid Crazy
Cupid's Bachelorette

Cupid Games
Return to Cupid Box Set Books 1-3
Cupid Help Me Box Set Books 4-6
Return to Cupid Box Set Books 7-9
Return to Cupid Box Set Books 10-12
**The Unlucky Bride

Contemporary Romance
My Sister's Boyfriend
The Wanted Bride
The Reluctant Santa
The Relationship Coach
Secrets, Lies, & Online Dating

Bride, Texas Multi-Author Series
**The Unlucky Bride

Coming Home for Christmas
I'll Be Home for Christmas
White Christmas
Santa's Baby
All I Want For Christmas
Box Set

Inheriting An Irish Groom
Inheriting a Scottish Castle

Kissing Oaks Billionaire Brothers
The Cowboy Billionaire's Lucky Break

The Cowboy Billionaire's Fate
The Cowboy Billionaire's Playbook
The Cowboy Billionaire's Secret
The Cowboy Billionaire's Deception
The Cowboy Billionaire's Match
Kissing Oaks Billionaire Brothers Box Set 1-3
Kissing Oaks Billionaire Brothers Box Set 4-6

Lipstick and Lead 2.0
Nailing the Hit Man
Nailing the Billionaire
Nailing the Single Dad
Box Set

Secrets of Mustang Island
Secrets of a Summer Place
Secrets of a Runaway Bride
Secrets From the Past
Secrets of a Reckless Life
Secrets of a Hidden Life
Secrets of a Midnight Letter

Secrets of Mustang Island Novellas
The Summer I Loved You
When We Meet Again
Christmas at Mustang Island

The Langley Legacy
Collin's Challenge

Short Sexy Reads
Racy Reunions Series
Paying For the Past
My Christmas Soldier
Cupid's Revenge

Western Historicals
A Hero's Heart
Second Chance Cowboy
Ethan

American Brides
**Katie: Bride of Virginia

Angel Creek Christmas Brides
**Charity
**Ginger
**Minne
**Cora
Angel Creek Christmas Box Set

Bad Girls of the West
Scandalous Sadie
Ravenous Rose
Tempting Tessa
Nellie's Redemption
Bad Girls Box Set

The Burnett Brides Series

The Rancher Takes A Bride
The Outlaw Takes A Bride
The Marshal Takes A Bride
The Christmas Bride
Boxed Set

Lipstick and Lead Series
Desperate
Deadly
Dangerous
Daring
Determined
Deceived
Defiant
Devious
Lipstick and Lead Box Set Books 1-4
Lipstick and Lead Box Set Books 5-9
Lipstick and Lead Box Set Books 1-9
**Quinlan's Quest

Mail Order Bride Tales
**A Brother's Betrayal
**Pearl
**Ace's Bride

Scandalous Suffragettes of the West
**Abigail
Bella
Mistletoe Scandal

Sylvia McDaniel is a USA Today Bestselling author with over one hundred western historical and contemporary romance novels under her belt. Known for creating memorable bad boys and good girls who can't help getting into trouble, she spends her days weaving compelling tales filled with heart, humor, and unexpected plot twists. Her family-oriented stories have earned her a loyal fanbase, and she's always dreaming up new ways to keep her readers hooked.

Married to her best friend for over thirty years, Sylvia recently relocated to Colorado, where she enjoys hiking and taking in the natural beauty of the forest that borders their home. Their spoiled dachshund, Zeus (who has his own column in her newsletter), and brat dog Bailey keeps them company on their adventures.

Though their grown son still resides in Texas, Sylvia keeps close ties to her southern roots, especially when it comes to football. A dedicated fan of both the Denver Broncos and the Dallas Cowboys, she's happiest when they're winning.

Love books? Love deals? Love a little mischief? Sign up for my Substack—it's free!
https://sylviamcdanielauthor.substack.com/
The End

9 781963 725148